Daughter
of the
Boyne

GW00372816

For Michael, Halvor and Erin Aakhus

'In the very earliest time, when both people and animals lived on earth, a person could become an animal if he wanted to, and an animal could become a human being. Sometimes they were people and sometimes animals, and there was no difference. All spoke the same language. That was the time when words were like magic. The human mind had mysterious powers. A word spoken by chance might have strange consequences. It would suddenly come alive and what people wanted to happen could happen – all you had to do was say it. Nobody could explain this; that's the way it was.'

Nalungiaq, Inuit tribe

'The wall of Paradise is built of contraries, nor is there any way to enter but for one who has overcome the highest spirit of reason who guards the gate.'

Nicholas of Cusa

Daughter
of the
Boyne

Patricia McDowell

Wolfhound Press

First Published 1992 by WOLFHOUND PRESS, 68 Mountjoy Square, Dublin 1 and Wolfhound Press (UK), 18 Coleswood Road, Harpenden, Herts AL5 1EQ

WOLFHOUND PRESS receives financial assistance from The Arts Council/An Chomhairle Ealaíon, Dublin, Ireland.

British Library Cataloguing in Publication Data
A catalogue record for this book is available from the British Library

ISBN 0-86327-349-1

Cover design: Fiona Lynch
Typesetting: WOLFHOUND PRESS
Printing: Cox and Wyman Ltd, Reading, England

Acknowledgments

Special thanks to Elizabeth Hickey, Mike Carson, François Camoin Seamus Cashman, Jean McMann, Sydney Lea, Michael Ryan, Tom Wilhelmus; and to the staff at Newgrange and Knowth.

CONTENTS

The People

The Daghdha, Lord of Uisnech, who keeps fair weather and harvest for Ireland

Bóinn, wife of Elcmhar, namesake of the River Boyne

Elcmhar, Lord of the Brugh on the Boyne, who tends the dead

Aonghus, son of the Daghda and Bóinn

Midhir, Lord of Brí Léith, the Daghda's grown son

Fuamnach, a sorceress, wife of Midhir, and foster-child of Bressal

Bressal, Sorcerer of Dowth

Ailill Horse-Rider, King of a northern horse people

Étaín Horse-Rider, his daughter

Eochaidh Airemh, a Laigin warrior, King of Tara and Dun Fremain

Ailill, his brother

Étar, a chieftain of the territory of Inber Cichmaine

Fedach, a druid

The Chief Places

The Brugh na Bóinne, Newgrange, Co. Meath

Dowth, Co. Meath

Uisnech, Co. Westmeath

Brí Léith (Slieve Golry), near Ardagh, Longford

Slievenamon, Co. Tipperary

Dun Fremain, Frewin Hill, Co. Westmeath

Tara, Co. Meath

The story begins about 1100 BC.

Of *The Wooing of Étaín*, Frank O'Connor wrote, 'It is one of the most beautiful stories in the world and must be older than almost anything else in Irish, for in it we see the early Celts living among the ruins of the Neolithic civilisations and wondering which gods were those who had occupied the country before them, cut down the woods, built causeways across the marshes, and erected great tombs like Newgrange for themselves....'

A Backward Look, Frank O'Connor

PROLOGUE

The Brugh na Bóinne

WHEN THE DAGHDHA wanted Bóinn, the wife of Elcmhar, he
harnessed his two grey stallions to his heavy oak-wheeled
chariot and drove to the Brugh. His chariot brought
thunder down into the oak woods from the hill of Uisnech,
thunder with the bright sun and the scarlet foxglove that
hung from every hedge and stone. Cattle and sheep ran
from the rough road before him, and crows flew above him,
screaming. He drove over the bogs, crushing new heather
and gold furze, sending mice and hare and badgers into
their tunnels. Sunlight and shadow rolled over the ground;
clouds broke and joined above him.

The River Boyne glittered below the mound of the
Brugh. In the field where Bóinn's white cattle grazed, he
unharnessed his horses and walked them slowly down to
the river to drink, for they were drenched with sweat from
the long drive. He himself walked into the water up to his

thighs, out into the middle where no man could stand with his head above the surface, where every year men drowned in the current. And he stood still and felt the weight and strength of the river moving down to the sea.

He swept the surface slowly with his hands, as swans and geese tread water. He felt the cold trickle running over rocks in the distant Mountain of the Hag, and the sharpness of quartz where water cuts a fine edge. He heard badgers and hedgehogs breathing in their nests beside the quick small stream, and otters slipping from a ledge smoothed by the widening brook. All went past him to the sea, through reeds bent in the fierce current, whipped under the water and streaming away, beautiful as a woman's long hair when she kneels, bathing in the river.

And he thought of Bóinn, of her low voice, her broad shoulders and long limbs, of her hair, loose, the color of winter rushes, and her eyes grey as the river when the wind stirs it. He knelt in the river, letting the reeds flow over his shoulders, and he stroked the river bed, his hand finding a smooth white rock, a gift for Bóinn, wife of Elcmhar, Lord of the Brugh.

He walked up the hill, through the circle of standing stones, their shadows sharp on the bright grass. All around the mound the great carved boulders lay end to end, holding the secrets of Elcmhar's craft. It was Elcmhar who tended the house of the dead, receiving them with food, shelter and comfort, so that they would remain and not disturb the living. For all things must come to the Brugh in the end, down to darkness, as rivers must flow to the sea. The Daghdha shuddered, having no wish to enter that dark place, but he loved the woman Bóinn, as he loved the river and sunlight, and he wanted her.

Elcmhar was rich with the payments of all who brought him their dead, but still he had sent the Daghdha no tribute that year. One-fifth of his cattle was the Daghdha's right as Lord of Uisnech, the centre of Ireland. Now Elcmhar appeared in the opening of the Brugh. His skin was stained with the greenish-black oils he ground from alder bark to disguise himself among the dead. A cape of starling feathers, black and iridescent, hung from his shoulders. He stood with one shoulder higher than the other, an elk's hoof bound with thongs to his left foot.

'If you come for tribute, I have nothing here to give you,' he said quickly. 'My cattle are on their summer pasture, on the hill of Slaine.'

'Still you owe me one-fifth of your herd,' answered the Daghdha, 'for the fair weather I have given you. Drive them here yourself this day, or find the river rising to your door.'

'Bóinn will not allow that to happen,' said Elcmhar, smiling. 'She can't betray me; it's against her nature.'

Bóinn looked at the Daghdha from behind Elcmhar, her eyes clear, her long straight hair with no adornment streaming over her grey cloak. He said softly, 'Go now, and return before nightfall with my cattle.'

'I will,' said Elcmhar. 'But Bóinn has much to do, and I'm afraid the Brugh will not accommodate you.' The passage into the chambers was narrow; a man of great size could not move his shoulders through.

'I'll wait for you beside the Boyne. Let neither hunger nor sleep take you. Go quickly so you are back by dark,' said the Daghdha, turning his back to the Brugh, looking down at the river.

Elcmhar climbed over the entrance stone, stared at his wife, then went quickly over the hill.

Beyond the river the Daghdha's horses had moved beside an old hawthorn tree in full flower. Their white tails were like the wings of some giant river bird, sweeping the ground. Wind moved through the grass where Bóinn's white cattle grazed, rippling the long grass like water about the legs of the cattle; two rivers below the Brugh, one blue of water, one green of earth.

The Daghdha turned and took Bóinn's hand, putting the small rock in her palm. 'A seed from the riverbed,' he said. 'Seeds need darkness to come alive.' She touched his shoulder, and he moved the great entrance stone aside, and entered the Brugh.

The sound of wind and crows stopped. The ground rose up into the dark, the passage narrowing ahead. Stones stood close together on each side, like trees growing from the floor to the roof of the passageway, stripped of bark with ringed scars where limbs had been cut away. The Daghdha put his palm flat against a carved spiral, and the rings grew, flowing out away from his hand. He moved slowly as through lake water, the stones giving way.

He saw the carved wide-open eyes of a small owl peer from its hole in the rock, the sign of forked lightning etched beside it; and beyond, a huge draped wing with each feather cut to lie upon the next. In the last pillar he felt the shape of a man's ribs, cold and smooth as death; then he took Bóinn's small hands, and she drew him into a chamber with a high corbelled ceiling.

He followed her to a smaller, lighted chamber. He lay down on the floor beside a white basin, smooth and bright as the moon, with the mark of rising and falling tide cut into its rim. Everywhere were the marks of water, on the walls, the roof; rings and rippled tides, waves and the crumpled, flowing lines of the sea when the surface is nearly still, but below all the movement of currents where living things and ocean forests collide and merge, collide and merge.

Bóinn knelt down beside him and put out the light.

And when he turned, putting his weight upon her, sinking deeply into her cool skin, a mist began to rise from the River Boyne. She took him with her mouth on his mouth, the mist growing, hiding the stallions of the Daghdha, shrouding the Brugh, covering the island. And the mist was so heavy on the hill of Slaine that Elcmhar didn't move, afraid because he could no longer tell where he walked. So he stopped and rested, waiting for the mist to break, but it grew thicker, and he couldn't tell if it was night or day around him.

In the Brugh the Daghdha loved Bóinn, and they made a truce of their desire. They had no fear of her husband while the mist covered the island. They talked of Bóinn's white cattle and the Daghdha's dun cattle, but never of Elcmhar or the rough urns of ash that stood in the corners of the chambers. He sang about the flowers hidden in the crevices of the stone land near the western sea, and of the gold that lay forgotten in the caves below. He sang of the sun on the hills of Uisnech that was his home; but he sang most often of the river, and how it was in every kind of light and weather and time of year.

The Daghdha held her for a night and a day, and for nine months, and held her hard as she bore a son to him. He wrapped the child in his cloak and laid him in the basin. They watched him sleep, and could not grow tired of watching him, but were anxious for him to wake so they could hold him, to touch his feet that had never touched earth, his fingers that clasped the rock that the Daghdha had brought from the river, pale as the shallows of the Boyne under a silver sky, grey and clear as the child's eyes.

He brought cows' milk and fed the child, so that Bóinn's milk would go from her breasts and not betray her. They called him Aonghus, the young son, because he was born between the brink of day and the fall of night, as the mist dissolved over the land, and Elcmhar turned back to the Brugh.

Then Bóinn gave the child to the Daghdha, and he covered him with his cloak, and went out into the wind and the dusk. He harnessed his horses to the chariot and drove west. When Elcmhar returned with his cattle, the Daghdha was a long way off. Night came, and the stars had not moved above the mound, because a year had passed in the Brugh while Ireland was cloaked in fog, and only the two who had loved and begotten a child knew that time had passed.

CHAPTER 1

Brí Léith — The Foster Child

WHEN MIDHIR SAW the Daghdha's chariot climbing his mountain fastness Brí Léith, he ordered his guards away from the road. Never before had the Lord of Uisnech come to Brí Léith without company or ceremony. No messenger had come ahead to warn Midhir of his father's approach.

'Let him seek me himself,' he said quickly to his chief guard. 'Don't stop him at the gate. But keep your weapons ready and watch the road. He may be followed.'

'If the Daghdha falls, the sky follows him,' whispered the guard.

Midhir went to the hall, and sat alone beside the fire, the great door standing open, but he didn't wait long. Soon the Daghda stood at the threshold, blocking the light. He came quietly into the room, closing the door softly, and Midhir, who had braced himself for rage, saw only gentleness in him. He sat down slowly beside the fire, and showed Midhir the sleeping child in his arms.

'He is Aonghus,' said the Daghdha. The baby started and woke.

Midhir touched the child's face.

'Will you keep him safe for me?' asked the Daghdha.

'The mountain will be lonely for him; we're quiet here, myself and Fuamnach. Won't he know his father, then?'

'He couldn't do better than Midhir, King of Brí Léith.'

'Someday he'll know you.'

'You of all my sons have the most wisdom,' said the Daghdha, touching Midhir's gold hair, then laying his hand on his shoulder, 'though you judge me most severely. He'll thrive here, in your reason. You'll teach him to bear loneliness. I don't have that skill.' He reached across the table and pulled a bowl of milk close, then dipped a cloth into it. He laid it on the baby's lips, and he drank, sucking on the cloth. 'Keep him hidden, Midhir, while he's helpless. Let him grow strong away from the world. But don't risk yourself in ignorance. It's Elcmhar I have offended, and his reach is great. Keep him far from Uisnech and the Brugh.'

'Elcmhar will know nothing. Aonghus will be my own son.'

'When you have children of your own body, don't forget him.'

Midhir laid the flat of a bronze blade against his arm. A fine line of blood rose up, then spread; he licked it. 'If the truth comes out,' he said, closing his eyes, 'he will still be my son.'

The Daghdha nodded. He knelt down before the fire, looking at the baby; his shadow covered the ceiling. 'He has her eyes.' He held the baby close to him. 'I won't see her again.' He put him into Midhir's arms. 'I thank you, Midhir, now.'

As he neared the door it swung open. Midhir turned, hiding the child with his body; then he saw that it was Fuamnach, his wife. She stared up at the Daghdha, her back against the wall. Her red hair was full with mist, and she wore a broad creased gold torc around her neck and a robe of silver-green wool with the pattern of willow leaves woven in it. Midhir saw that the elegance of her dress was no accident, nor was the intrusion; but now the excuse for entering was lost. She couldn't speak for fear of him. The Daghdha looked at her and went out through the door, into the rain.

From that time, Midhir raised Aonghus as his own son on the mountain Brí Léith that stood alone above the plains and bogs. Midhir's house rose up from a mound on the mountain like an ancient ash, circled by a rath of quartz. There was a high dark door of yew with bronze latches, and windows that looked east over the pines, bogs and tulachs, the phantom lakes that come and go; and the plains and oak woods that stretched to Uisnech, and the Brugh, and the sea beyond. For seventeen years Aonghus knew himself as Midhir's son, and he had great skill at hurling and with horses.

But one day at hurling Aonghus insulted the captain of the opposing team, the boy Triath of the Fir Bolg, and Triath told Aonghus what he had himself overheard, that Aonghus was no son of Midhir's flesh. Then Midhir took the boy aside and told him all he knew, and that he himself would take Aonghus to meet his father.

That night, when everything had been prepared for the ride to Uisnech at daybreak, Midhir saw that Aonghus could not be content in his company, that words came hard to him now out of anger and loyalty. So he went down to Fuamnach's house in the woods below the rath.

When he had brought her from Dowth, where she had been the foster-child of the sorcerer Bressal Etarlam, to Brí Léith to be his wife, he had made her a small house in the woods, beside a stream. From the open door Midhir saw her sitting beside the fire, her dark red hair loose and crumpled from its braids. She was stretching a goatskin over a taut circle of stripped rowan and binding it with thongs, making a bodhran. He thought it would be good to lie with her, and that from this time there might be peace between them.

When she saw him she got up from the chair, leaning the drum against the hearth.

'I'm disturbing you,' said Midhir.

'You are not. For myself, I wouldn't have given the child away,' she said, handing him wine, then pushing the hair away from her face with her white forearm. She sat down on the hearth, holding her own cup with both hands, her grey eyes on him. 'And it's Elcmhar touching her now; that I would not bear.'

'He has no choice. He knows it would be unwise to make an enemy of Elcmhar,' said Midhir. 'I doubt that Elcmhar himself could hold Uisnech even if he could take it, but there are others, more ambitious, who would go with him against the Daghdha, hoping for their own chance. The Daghdha must be cautious.'

Fuamnach stared at him. 'And give you the risk, instead. Elcmhar won't thank you for your part in this. Today the secret comes out of a stranger's mouth. Tomorrow how many will trust you?'

'It's time the father knew the son.'

'The Daghdha is your father, too. You're closer to him than anyone. Still he puts you in danger.'

'It's no danger. He'll acknowledge Aonghus for Bóinn's sake; but he will also protect her and himself. There's much at stake.'

Fuamnach set her cup on the hearth and came to him, sitting on his lap with her arms around his neck. 'And Uisnech will be safe. I think you would lose your land for love,' she said softly, and kissed him. Midhir moved his hands under her cloak, touching her bare skin. Fuamnach whispered, kissing his eyes, 'Oh, I love your eyes; they are the colour of the pine forest, of the kingfisher's wings; I love your black brows, your gold hair. Will you be Lord of Uisnech?'

Midhir took hold of her arms, held her apart from him. Her hair fell over her eyes. 'Is that what you want, Fuamnach?'

She threw her head back and looked straight at him. 'You want it yourself. You know the Daghdha favours you. If he has become careless, then the time is right for you to take his place.'

'I've no wish to see Brí Léith destroyed.'

'I don't believe you.' She stood up. 'You won't tell me what you're planning. Why do you hate me?'

'I don't hate you, Fuamnach.' Heaviness lay on him, as if he had marched all day in the rain and found no battle. 'I don't want to take my father's land.'

'You love the mountain and your solitude, Midhir, and nothing more.'

'Be still, Fuamnach.'

'I am not what you imagined, am I, Midhir? Bressal's brilliant student. You wanted me because you thought I cared for loneliness better than anything; better than you. How generous you were to make this house, so that I'd sleep alone, rather than beside you.'

'You're very clever, Fuamnach. I have always thought so.'

'I am not. I have no trap to bind you. Where is the net, the tether?' She laughed. 'I think you would gnaw off your own leg to get free, if you believed you were held against your will.'

He stepped forward, to touch her.

She backed away. 'Midhir, what will you do if the Daghdha doesn't acknowledge him? It'll be your shame, then, and mine. If you go against the Daghda for the sake of this boy, and you will, being proud, you'll be alone. Your brothers would be glad to see your head on a stake beside the gate of Uisnech. Don't do this to me. I've done nothing these years but love you, and use everything I know to keep you safe. You think the beast will mind you out of love. But I say it is only because it knows it's being watched that it doesn't turn on you.'

'Hush, Fuamnach. There's no sense in you.'

'Don't you dare laugh at me, Midhir. It's you who are foolish. There is no passion in you.'

He stepped toward her quickly, and she cried out and ran to the door.

'I'm not going to hurt you, Fuamnach,' said Midhir. He would have struck her if she had not cried out first.

'Tell the truth, Midhir,' she said. He saw the fear of him still in her eyes. 'Answer me this: when will you love me?'

'Why do you ask questions that have no answers?'

'Then what shall I ask? Where have you gone today, Midhir? What woman have you covered?'

Midhir walked past her, out the door. He heard her voice, after him, 'No, you can't love me. It's true. I knew it. Bressal didn't want me to marry you. He knew the coldness of beautiful Midhir.'

CHAPTER 2

Uisnech – The Daghdha's Throne

IT WAS STILL DARK when Midhir touched the boy's shoulder. Aonghus came awake at once, dressed quickly, and they went outside. There were stars above Brí Léith as they drove their chariots single-file down the mountain. Side by side they flew along the high ridges of bog, with gold harness fittings and two dark grey horses before each set of light-spoked, fast-turning wheels. There were bronze shields bound to the rails, and gold hilted spears with slicing blades beside them. Twenty warriors on horseback followed them on the road to Uisnech.

When they reached the Cold Lake, Midhir showed Aonghus the hills of Uisnech in the distance. By midday, as they passed into the Daghdha's land, the sun kindled everything afire: green grass, bronze cattle and yellow furze. Guards stopped them where the road joined a narrow track up into the hills, the way to the Daghdha's fort. They bowed to Midhir, recognizing him instantly, and to the strange young warrior beside him.

They rode through a tunnel of hawthorn with grey and twisted trunks. At the end of the track they came to a gate, where they left their horses and began the climb to the fort, hidden in the folds of the hills. On the first ridge a bull came towards them, shaking his gigantic horns. Midhir set his staff into the ground; the bull stopped and stood quietly, his head low, and drowsy with sun. Midhir and Aonghus walked on past him through the herd of cows.

They crossed rolling pastures and streams until they reached the fort at the foot of the eastern slope of Uisnech, where the granite throne marked the centre of Ireland. The gate was crowded with people dressed in bright clothes, selling food, animals and bronze, playing music. They passed through the gate, crossed a black stream, climbing the steep rise to the white standing stones that circled the Daghdha's chair like a crown.

There was a blast of sun and wind at the top of the hill.

Midhir saw the Daghdha look at Aonghus, at the hard streaks of muscle in the arm that held the shaft of a perfect bronze spear, at the boy's steady grey eyes with the light and shadow of crystal of Midhir's mountain realm in them, at Bóinn's chestnut hair. 'Who is this boy who has never come until now?'

Midhir stepped forward. 'Here is Aonghus grown to manhood. He wishes that his father acknowledge him and that land be given to him; that is the birthright of any man or woman. It's not right that he has nothing when his father is the king of Uisnech.'

The Daghdha shifted in his stone seat; sun and shadow reeled over the grass and the granite. 'He's welcome,' he said, his clear blue eyes fixed on Midhir. 'He is my son. But the land I have for him is not yet vacant.'

'What land is that?' asked Midhir.

'The Brugh na Bóinne.'

Midhir looked off to the east. A blue line, clouds or sea, marked the rim of the land. 'And who is there?' he asked softly.

'Elcmhar is there, and I have no wish to annoy him.'

Midhir put his hand lightly on Aonghus's shoulder. 'Then, Aonghus, you and I shall find a way to take it.'

'Aonghus, go alone to the Brugh na Bóinne,' said the Daghdha. 'On Samhain, when the dead visit the living, and no man carries weapons, Elcmhar goes into the mound of the Brugh, unarmed, except for a stick of white hazel. You must be well armed. And if Elcmhar submits to you, don't kill him.

'This is your demand. You shall be Lord of the Brugh for a day and a night. And if you keep the Brugh for a day and a night, don't give it up to Elcmhar afterwards. Force Elcmhar to come to me. Then I'll hear their arguments and make judgement.'

Midhir turned to Aonghus. The boy bowed to them both and left them. The Daghda signalled his guards, and the hill was quickly cleared of people.

'Sit beside me awhile, Midhir. Tonight I'll send a storm into the valley of the Boyne.' He picked up his harp and struck a chord; the wind dropped.

'River, where the bones of mountains
Are washed and made new,
Where wrens sing loud
Hidden in your weeds,
Remember now.
One night I stood above you,
High above your banks,
On the mound of dark and watched
While you slept, the child in your arms;

The mist rising and the new lamb safe.
Two swans drifted sleeping behind the reeds,
And there, in the middle of the river,
The reeds lay smooth, swept
By your dreams moving slowly out to sea.
While she dreams we are safe, we drift;
The nights will not be counted,
But soon we will be apart and changed.
Now thunder drums in the west,
Faint pulse of the bodhran;
It is the distant sound of my horses,
Going away to find the battle.
Follow, darkness,
Let the heavy cloud rest on this hill above the river
And weep;
The swans will sleep together below the Ford,
But I will never hear the wind
And the water moving down to the sea,
Or wade through her dreams.
I will never stand on the mound and sing.
Fall gently, rain, into her dreams.
Soft river under the storm, show her his eyes, grey,
His hair the colour of winter reeds bent under the
water.
Awake, Bóinn, my love,
Hear the rain on your roof of earth and stone,
Aonghus is coming now,
He is coming.'

As he sang clouds began to gather above Uisnech.

'It's not my hope that she will leave Elcmhar, for she will not,' said the Daghdha, gazing east, where the sky had grown dark. 'If the boy is successful then I'll build her a house of light on a high bluff above the river, and Elcmhar will live there with her.' He turned to Midhir. 'You've raised the boy well, Midhir. He's not fearful.'

'It's his own nature. But I've kept him on the mountain, hidden, and he has never challenged a man of Elcmhar's craft.' The Daghdha didn't answer, so Midhir left him and found Aonghus, and they drove home to Brí Léith. Midhir gave him a dagger with a curved blade and a hilt of gold, and a long sword that wouldn't break the cloak and give him away. On the eve of Samhain he sent Aonghus on his own stallion to the Brugh. Then he went into the mound below his house to wait for the passing of the treacherous night, and for word from the boy.

CHAPTER 3

The Trick of Samhain

AONGHUS FOLLOWED THE BOYNE along the south bank, watching the current as the river appeared in the breaks of alder, willow and reeds. The tide came up from the sea below the mound of Dowth, Midhir had told him. There he could rest his horse and Bressal would give him food and drink. From the mound he could see the Brugh from safe vantage, before anyone might see him.

When Bressal opened the door of his house to Aonghus he stared beyond him at the dappled stallion with blood-red face and frowned. He was a big man, with silver hair to his shoulders, light eyes and gruff voice. 'Where did you steal that horse? From Midhir?'

'Midhir and Fuamnach greet you and send you these herbs. I am Aonghus, of Brí Léith. I have a message for Elcmhar of the Brugh.'

'You are Midhir's kin; you have his look. There's a well below. Get water for your horse. You can leave him to graze if he'll not run off. There are no mares close by.'

When Aonghus returned, Bressal was sitting on a flat stone, gently shaking the roots of the plants apart. 'Are you Fuamnach's son?' he asked.

Aonghus shook his head.

'It's twenty years since I saw her last. Is she an old woman now with ten children?'

'She's beautiful. There's no age on her.'

'Well. Fuamnach loves Midhir still. And you have a message for Elcmhar on Samhain. What could that be? Don't worry, boy, I'll leave it in you. You'll come back and tell me news of Brí Léith when your message is delivered and your tongue loose again. Now come up the mound and I'll show you the Brugh, so you won't get lost before dark.'

Aonghus stood on the hill and looked east, where Bressal pointed. There was a white hill on the horizon. 'Keep the river on your left,' said Bressal. 'There'll be no gates closed against you tonight. No weapons, no trespassers. But bonfires to frighten a stallion. Go straight to the mound. Elcmhar's house stands empty tonight; he'll sleep inside the Brugh. And I in the mound of Dowth.' He touched the knife blade under Aonghus's cloak. 'You're not afraid of ghosts or hazel wands? Take care, boy, what you do tonight. Samhain is a wave that travels through the year. Go on. When Elcmhar is in his trance he won't talk to anyone, not even one who is kin to his wife. You have her eyes, boy.'

When Aonghus reached the Brugh he walked his horse to the top of the grassy mound, and tied him to the single pillar that stood there. The sun lay on the hill beyond the river, and the stone cast a long shadow towards Dowth.

A large boulder lay before the entrance of the Brugh; it was as long as two men lying head to foot, and as high as his waist. Two carved waves burst from the bottom of the stone; they seemed to erupt from the ground, from the centre of the hill, rooted deeply in earth. The waves rolled, spreading east and west, coiling into great spirals that whirled in the centre, storm clouds in the heavens. From the top a deeply carved vertical shaft was drawn into the central spiral. Waves broke along the upper edge. Crystals grew from the outer rims of the spirals; quartz covered the ground before the entrance.

Aonghus climbed over the stone, and entered the Brugh.

The wind stopped; the passage was dark. He felt his way along with his hands. There was a distant sound of water, a soft splashing. He came to the end of the passage, and into a dim room with a high, corbelled ceiling. Three small chambers led off from it; two were dark; a woman knelt in the third chamber beside a lamp. She was washing bones in a shallow basin.

Aonghus tapped the hilt of his knife on the stone beside him. She turned, startled. Her white hands froze above the basin. Her eyes were light.

'Are you Bóinn?' he whispered.

A voice came from another chamber. 'Woman, why do you disturb me? Be silent.'

Aonghus stepped back out of the light. 'I am Aonghus,' he said.

Then suddenly Elcmhar stood in the central chamber with a white hazel wand in his hand, pale as distant lightning. Bóinn moved slowly in front of the lamp; the chamber grew darker.

'Who is it? Speak again,' said Elcmhar, his voice hoarse. 'Show yourself. Who are you? Who are you looking for?'

Aonghus didn't answer.

Elcmhar turned slowly, reaching out with his hazel wand, testing the dark. He whispered, 'Speak, spirit! What do you want?'

Aonghus moved quickly. He caught Elcmhar's arms and feathered cape behind him, and pressed the flat of his knife against his throat. The hazel wand fell to the ground.

'You're trespassing on my land,' said Aonghus. He heard Midhir's deep, fierce voice.

'Who are you?' whispered Elcmhar.

'Your death, this moment, unless you leave.'

'I can't see you, my Death.'

'I am Lord of the Brugh. Yield this place for the night and the day after, and I'll let you live.'

'I yield,' he said quickly.

'Swear,' said Aonghus.

'I swear.'

'Then get out!' Aonghus turned him to the passage, and let go of him. He watched Elcmhar's shadow move between the stones until he was gone.

His mouth was dry; he drank from a flask beside the basin. It was bitter. He leaned against the wall of the chamber. The corbelled ceiling spun slowly.

'Sit down,' said Bóinn, drying the bones with a cloth. 'The drink will make you weak.'

He sat down beside her. Her lamp sputtered; the oil was almost gone. Aonghus touched a spiral carved in the chamber wall.

'The skin has all been stripped away,' she said, watching him. Her eyes were light grey, like his own. 'Bones must be clean before they're burned. Only trees who lose their leaves can blossom again.' She laid the bones carefully down upon the cloth. 'I would say they'd belonged to a fox, wouldn't you? He was small, that child.' She put her cool hand on his face. 'Aonghus,' she said softly, 'don't be afraid.'

'Tomorrow Elcmhar will see that I'm flesh and blood.'

'Your father has given you the Brugh.'

'Is it his to give?'

'You don't know what is in his mind,' said Bóinn.

'My inheritance is stolen property,' said Aonghus. His pointed anger kept the room from spinning. 'The generosity of a father to his son.'

'This place will belong to you.' She touched his hair, his jaw. 'Aonghus, sleep has been kind. In my dreams I'd kept you. And now, at last, now, when you've come back, I must go.' She took his hand, and put a pale stone on his palm, and closed his fingers around it. 'The Daghdha put this in your hand the day you were born.'

'Tomorrow they'll have weapons,' said Aonghus, his voice flat. He stared into the fire beside the basin. He watched the flames lick over the stone rim, over the surface of the water. The rings on the ceiling were spreading; water and flames poured over the sides of the basin.

Bóinn's voice seemed to come from behind him now. 'That you see hunger doesn't mean that love does not exist. The Brugh is yours, if you hold it.'

He opened his hand and looked at the small stone. It was dark blue. 'Mother, do you see –' he looked up. There was no answer. The lamp went out. The chamber was completely dark. He felt his way along the passageway, hands braced against the stones on each side. The air changed; there was a brush of wind on his face.

He saw the silver edge of the entrance stone. Like a huge sleeping dog, it lay across the opening, guarding the Brugh. He stepped out into the night. The sky was clear. There were faint lights in the river below. There was no one out. The house beside the river was dark. Cattle lay motionless in the grass and his horse grazed alone on the top of the mound. He went back into the passage, lay down close to the wall, pulled his cloak over him and slept.

The next evening, when Aonghus came out of the Brugh, he saw men with swords and spears and Elcmhar with a long pike for killing pigs. Farmers, women and children stood behind them with stones ready to throw at him. But when they saw him they only stared.

Elcmhar choked, cried out, 'Who is this boy?'

'I am Aonghus,' he said. 'The Brugh is mine. I do not give it back.'

Elcmhar said, 'The boy is mad. Who are his kin?'

'The land is mine,' said Aonghus. 'My horse has grazed this land and no one has challenged me. Do you deny what you swore, Elcmhar? You trespass here.'

Elcmhar turned to the crowd, and his voice shook with anger. 'Get him out of there. He has desecrated a sacred place with his trick.' The people didn't move. He swung his spear toward Aonghus. 'Come out, boy. The eve of Samhain is past, and my patience ended.'

'Let the Daghdha judge the outcome. You gave up the Brugh; now I hold it. You can't take it from me without judgement.'

'Let the Daghdha judge,' cried the people. And they said that Elcmhar must go to Uisnech for judgment, because he had given up his land to save his own life. Twelve men were chosen from them to hold the Brugh until the Daghdha had made his decision, and twelve more followed Aonghus to Uisnech to protect him.

Midhir stood with Aonghus and Elcmhar on Uisnech as the Daghdha gave judgment. 'If a man lets his horse graze on certain pasture for a day and a night,' said the Daghdha, 'and no one drives him from the land, then the land is his for all time. Elcmhar gave the land freely as hostage for his own safety, for the night and the day, and so it shall belong to Aonghus for all time, for it is in days and nights that the world is spent. But Aonghus must not harm Elcmhar as long as he lives, for that was the price of his land.

'Elcmhar, you will not be without land, for I'll give you land as fine as the Brugh, land that lies along the River Boyne on the east bank, land that I have kept. That land is Cleitech, the high plateau that looks down on the Brugh and Knowth and with that land I give you all the gifts of the Boyne, salmon and rich pasture, and fields for the games of Samhain. It shall be yours as long as you live, and afterwards the place shall be hidden, so your bones will be safe from your enemies, but your name shall be remembered. That is my judgment. Will you answer it, Elcmhar?'

'I will take Cleitech and build a fort there,' said Elcmhar. 'With my wife Bóinn, I'll live above the river, and take tribute. But if the boy trespasses upon my land, I'll kill him.'

'Go then, if you're satisfied. Aonghus, don't speak to him or trouble him further.'

That night Midhir brought Aonghus to his camp on the shore of the Cold Lake, and Fuamnach met them with wine and oat cakes from the hearths of Brí Léith. They cooked mutton wrapped in straw, steeped in a vat of lake water, heated with stones. Fuamnach laughed, talking of Bressal. She knelt behind Midhir to pour his wine, wrapping her arms around his neck, her cloak falling over his shoulders. He rubbed his face against her smooth arm, and smiled at Aonghus, then he looked away, at the dark lake.

Aonghus said, 'When will you come to the Brugh, Midhir?'

'Within the year.'

'Come soon. What will the people say if my own foster father won't be my guest?'

'Aonghus,' said Fuamnach. 'When will you be a man? You must hold your land yourself. Midhir has risked enough for you. What are you afraid of?' She stood up and put a branch on the fire. 'Death can come anytime. The boar waits in the forest, Aonghus, his mane-ridge stiff, and his tusks polished; he waits for the day you walk without your weapons. The wolf waits for the new lambs. They are very patient.

'This is my advice to you, boy. Watch the shadows, and learn their shapes, every leaf and branch and stone. They never lie. Look carefully, in all weather, and soon you'll know who comes where and when, and nothing will happen that you didn't know before its time.'

Midhir stirred the fire with a stick. A spark rose, then the ash curled and floated away. 'Fuamnach, the wind bends the tree. You are not the wind. You must leave it.'

'Leave the gate open, let in the wolf. I look for holes in the hedge. I can protect my own, if I'm careful. If someone will listen to me, and not be a fool.'

'You watch the dark, Fuamnach, you'll see disaster in it.'

'I will watch.'

'Then look!' He drove his staff into the fire and sparks flew. There was sudden, loud thunder. Lightning lit up the lake and the woods around them. Everything in the forest was clear, sharp as bright day. Under the trees owls carried off small rabbits, their necks limp, foxes tore apart the bodies of mice and voles. A wolf lapped blood from the neck of a spotted fawn. Worms crawled over the trees, chewing leaves. Beneath the lake fish ate from a rotting human head.

Fuamnach stood still, her hands on her face. Her voice was small, shaking. 'What are you doing, Midhir? Stop it! Stop it! Make it dark.'

The woods were only black shapes again, and Midhir took his staff out of the ash. 'There. We'll live forever. Be glad.'

'You will never love, Midhir,' she said, and walked behind the fire.

'Before next Samhain, I'll come,' he said to Aonghus.

'Do you swear it?'

'I swear it. Now sleep; it's late. We have work tomorrow.'

Then Fuamnach screamed. Midhir turned and saw that her cloak was on fire. She fumbled with the brooch that held it fastened around her neck, but couldn't open it. He reached her, grabbed the collar of the cape and ripped it apart.

He carried her away from the burning wool. When he put her down she kept her face hidden against his chest, crying. 'Midhir, walk with me.' He took her hand and they walked along the lake. When the campfire was a distant blur she stopped and turned toward him; her eyes still wet. 'Don't go, Midhir. Not for a year.' She put her hands in his hair, and brought his mouth to hers. She moved her hands inside his cloak and swept the length of his body, touching the long muscle of his thigh, the hollow at his hip that curved up across his stomach, flowing over the muscles of his chest, kissing the hollow in his throat. He lowered her to the ground and kissed her, seeing her green eyes, nearly closed, watching him.

By the fire, Aonghus heard the lake lapping the stones, and dreamed of his mother's face over the white basin, waves moving across the water that she gently stroked. He woke, turning toward the lake, and watched the dark waves come in. They were soft now, and nearly smooth, with no light in them at all.

CHAPTER 4

The Wounding of Midhir

THE DAY WAS BRIGHT when Midhir rode with his guards to the Brugh to stay with Aonghus. They crossed the wet land where few cattle grazed, their horse's hooves black from turf and the heather, burned off for pasture. The land belonged to the Daghda, so Midhir rode ahead at his own pace, letting his guards take their time with the carts and cattle over the bog.

When he reached the hard ground of Meath, he stopped beside a well to let his horse drink, to wash its hooves, and to wait for his guard. He changed the plain bridle for one with gold fittings that flashed against the granite-coloured stallion. As he dipped his flask into the well the water quivered. His horse raised his head from the grass. There was a drumming sound. Midhir grabbed the horse's rein.

A herd of mares and foals ran into the field across the stream and his stallion neighed and reared, jerking the rein out of his hand. He took off, running back and forth along the riverbank. A white stallion came out of the woods on the far side of the water. His mane flared from his high curved neck, and his tail spread out behind him. There was a girl on his back, holding him reined tightly, leading a chestnut mare. He saw Midhir's stallion and reared. Midhir caught his horse's trailing lead and mounted him, turning him in circles, driving him back to the well.

The girl got off her horse, unbuckled his bridle and let him go. He reared, kicked, then turned towards the mares, and trotted, floating across the field towards them. He reached the closest mare, and touched her chest. She wheeled and kicked and the herd began to move as one beast, running with the stallion.

The girl rode the chestnut mare across the stream to Midhir. Her hair was yellow gold, plaited in three braids, as a child wears them. She nodded her thanks.

'There'll be good foals next summer by that stallion,' said Midhir. 'I might want to buy one. Whose horses are they?'

'Mine,' she said. Her eyes were bright blue under dark brows. She wore only a light sleeveless tunic, split at the sides. Her legs were bare, and it seemed to Midhir that her skin cast light on the leaves and branches of the woods around them.

He reached over and stroked the mare's neck. She twitched under his hand at first, as if it were a fly, then grew still. 'Who is your father?' he asked.

A crow screamed and took off from a tree nearby and the horses shied. They brought their horses side by side again.

'My father's Ailill Echraide, king of Ulster. He pays tribute to the Daghda for this winter pasture, and I have brought the horses here at Samhain for many years now. But they're my horses,' she answered laughing. 'I am Étaín Echraide, Horse-Rider. And you are Midhir of Bri Leith, far from home. I recognized you.' She dismounted, and led her horse to the well to drink.

He slipped down off his horse, and followed her. 'I took you for a groom. I would have remembered you. Such beauty and skill should be famous.' He stroked his stallion's leg, then slowly picked up his hoof, and carved the mud away with a twig. When he was finished he dropped his foot, patting the horse's shoulder. 'So you won't sell me your stallion, Étaín?'

She shook her head, smiling, running her hand over his stallion's soft nose and mouth.

'Where's your company?' she asked.

'My guards follow me.'

'Are you travelling far?'

'To the Brugh na Bóinne.'

'That is your road then,' she said, pointing towards the path that ran east from the well. ' And mine is north tonight.'

'You're not afraid to ride alone on Samhain?' he asked.

'Are you trying to frighten me?'

'If I were your father I'd watch you closely.'

'Then I'm very glad that you're not,' she laughed. ' Be careful that you don't lose your way,' she said, bringing her horse around the well to mount her.

Midhir held the mare's reins. 'And you never get lost?'

Étaín grew still, her right hand laid lightly on the mare's withers. He saw her shoulders rise with a deep breath. She looked down at her left hand; her fingers barely touched the reins beside his hand. 'My horses know the way. All beasts can find their way home.' She looked up at him. Her eyes were like sapphire and jet. 'I think it's only man who strays from the place he marks as his own and is lost. All else is wild and dangerous to him.

'Swans find their way home,' she said, taking the reins in both hands, her fingers holding them lightly as a pipe, a dry reed, and looking away. 'Winter's coming; the dark comes early, and seeds are scarce. They grow restless and one day they're high above the clouds. They fly where they must, because one mountain, one island feels right and another false. The moon is bright and lakes shine below in the dark. The clouds are full of wind and rain, but they keep on. Then one day they fly low over the trees, and they hear the larks and the river and they're heavy and tired, so they skim into the water. And they've come home.' She looked down, suddenly embarrassed. 'Where do you ride tonight, Midhir?'

'To the Brugh,' he said quietly.

She nodded. 'I asked you before.'

He covered her hand with his own. 'Walk with me awhile, Étaín. There's an old orchard not far from here, just beyond the trees, if I'm right. The Dagdha planted it long ago. Not far at all.'

They followed a deer track, ducking under branches with ripe black sloes, red berries on the hawthorn and holly. Midhir's cloak got caught on a holly bush and they stopped to untangle it. Further on he stopped again beside an oak that had a patch of bark rubbed off; he put his hand over the raw trunk. On the forest floor around them leaves and moss had been scraped away, showing the bare soil.

'We're trespassing,' said Étaín softly.

'Look there,' said Midhir. 'Do you see him?'

In the orchard beyond the oaks a big stag, his neck thick with the rut, his antlers smooth, fed on apples from the lowest branches. Midhir gave his horse's reins to Étaín, stepped quietly out and pulled apples from a tree, then moved back.

'There's something in the woods over there,' he whispered, touching Étaín's arm, cool and soft as a moth's wing.

He took the horses' reins and backed them from the edge of the meadow. They watched.

Wolves moved slowly at the far end of the clearing. The stag looked up just as one came fast straight toward him. He lowered his crown. As the first swerved off, the stag turned his head, watching him, and a second leaped to his throat. The third attacked from behind, snapping at his ankles, severing tendons. As the stag began to sink the wolf in front tore the jugular, and one at each side of him ripped open his chest. The stag went down hard, and didn't stir. The wolves lapped the blood, and fed quietly, watching the woods.

'So fast,' said Étaín, her hands on the mare's neck and head, holding her. 'He's careless, showing himself in bright day.'

'He could not be otherwise at Samhain,' said Midhir. 'Desire was on him and loneliness drove him into the open.'

'Winter's coming; it'll soon be dark,' she said and turned back into the forest. They followed the track of broken branches. In the slanted light the oaks were gold; beyond the thorn trees the well and the stream glittered.

'There's a swan flying above us,' said Midhir, coming up behind her.

She stopped. 'I see it now.'

His hands rested lightly on her shoulders. 'Like the dead, they are, coming back tonight to places they knew in life.' He could see the shape of her bones, like wings, under her skin.

'In dreams I fly above the plains and sea,' she said softly. 'Sometimes I can't find my way back. There's no place to land, and I wake. Perhaps that's what death is like.' She blew into her hands; steam rose in the air. ' We shouldn't speak of such things on Samhain. I feel the nameless ones gathering.'

'It's nothing, only dusk and cold coming,' he said, his voice low. His hands cupped her bare shoulders. He moved his hands, palms flat, down her smooth arms, and up again, to warm them. 'Come with me now, Étaín, to the Brugh. I'll keep you safe. Tonight while we lie together the swans fly south to Slievenamon, to the hill of women, who wind their spindles of white swan's down that turn the wheel of the moon, so that men can see it rise and fall. And every woman and every mare is wound by their spindle, while they can bear young, and the wheel turns in their sleep and in their dreams, and no man can find it, except at his death, so he scratches it on stone.' Gently he unfastened the gold thong that bound her braid.

'What are you doing?' she whispered.

'I want to see your beautiful hair loose.'

She turned and he caught her hands.

'Come with me tonight, Étaín, *Bé Find,* my bright woman.'

She shook her head, taking her hands from his. She laid one palm gently against his chest for a moment, then withdrew it, and stroked the mare's copper neck.

He knelt down beside the well, bringing an apple from his cloak. He split it on his five-pointed spear. The horses came to him and he gave them pieces from his open hand.

'She likes them, too.'

'She does.'

He divided another apple on the bronze point. His stallion nudged his arm. 'Be patient. You must share.' He said lightly, 'Come to the Brugh, Étaín, and we'll play fidchell.'

'For what stakes?'

'Let the winner name them,' he answered, and laughed.

'I'd better not play fidchell with you. I'd rather sell you a horse.'

'You're wise not to trust me,' he said.

'Nothing is forbidden to the oak king and his lightning. They trespass on every land. He takes whatever he wants.'

'I'm no horse raider. I pay gold for my stallions.' He looked across the stream; the white horse chased the mares.

'I could not refuse you; though there's not enough gold on Meath to buy him,' said Étaín. 'Someday I'll give him away.' She climbed up on her mare, and turned her toward the north road. The mare threw her head down and back, pacing. 'Perhaps I'll have a horse for you, Midhir. How would I find you then?'

Midhir caught her rein; the mare stamped and stood still, breathing the sweet fragrant juice on his hands. 'Fly west and you'd see one mountain alone on the dark plain. The fort is quartz stone. In sunlight it shines like ice; at night it glows with the bonfire. Fly below the clouds and you'll not miss it.'

She smiled at him. Her mouth was red as hawthorn berries.

'So you're going to leave me, then,' he said.

'I am.'

He took an apple out of his cloak and held it out to her. 'The first rule of fidchell: if you take my apple, then I must return your rowan queen. I give you this freely, and let you go on your way. But first you must give me something in return.'

Étaín took the apple; then she quickly slipped from the horse and knelt beside the well. She brought water dripping from her white hands to him. Midhir drank from her hands, then kissed them.

Then she was suddenly mounted, and turning the mare in a circle, her gold braids following the movement of her shoulders. She stopped the mare dead still beside him. She leaned over and kissed him on the mouth. She said softly, ' Be careful tonight, that the ghosts don't take you for a lover, for I've never seen a man with eyes like yours.' Then she sat up straight, and held up one hand in salute, smiling to him, and then the mare moved out, and Étaín was gone.

The woods were still. The ground was covered with violet self-heal, their petals stamped into the ground by the horses' hooves. Midhir picked up a crushed flower. The delicate blossom had much power. Those who went to battle in the summer when it bloomed often carried it with them, for dressing wounds; but it was late for the *ceannbhan beag* to be in flower. He heard the sound of carts and horses coming. He climbed on his horse and waited for his guards to ride on together.

The sun was low when they reached the Brugh. Torches ringed the two low raths on each side of the river. Midhir found Aonghus and his company watching stallions fighting on the opposite bank, the rath enclosed by dense holly hedges to keep the animals from escaping. A horse from the Brugh and a horse from Cleitech fought, and as Midhir reached Aonghus, the Cleitech horse killed the other, and there was a lull while the victor was captured and the body dragged from the arena. The anger on Aonghus's face left when he saw Midhir, and he stood up, crying aloud that Midhir had come, giving him the place of honour. Servants came up with wine and food, and soon the hurling match began, the last contest between the warriors of Cleitech and the Brugh. Below the fort of Cleitech, under a roofed palisade, Elcmhar watched with his company.

The Cleitech team scored quickly. 'We've got to move out of our own territory,' mumbled Aonghus. 'We're being too cautious.'

'The sun's going down,' said Midhir.

'Watch...it's dark and our men get hurt. Elcmhar thinks we can't see. He took his time with the ceremonies. Dusk comes to his advantage; the enemy knows its own ground. We should be playing on this side of the river. Now look!' Aonghus stood up and screamed. 'Did you see him strike our man? Did you see that?' The player was lying on the ground, and the man from Cleitech raised the ball up on his stick. 'The ball was right in front of him! Stop the game!'

Three men from the Brugh knocked the player down. The game turned into a brawl, ash sticks flashing. Aonghus moved down through the crowd toward the river, cursing Elcmhar, and Midhir followed him. At the riverbank he caught Aonghus, grabbed his arm, and pulled him around to face him. The boy's eyes shone with wine.

'He wants to shame me in front of you,' said Aonghus, breathing hard. 'I'll kill him for it. I'm not afraid of him. Do you think I'm afraid of him?'

Guards from Cleitech were running down the hill towards the field.

'Don't move from this place,' said Midhir. 'I'll go and end it. You do just what Elcmhar hopes. Let him see you stay here now.'

Midhir took a horse and galloped across the ford below Cleitech. He felt the horse pull back as they came near the ring of torches, but he drove him through the lights and they cleared the hedge, landing close to the brawl. The men scattered before the big horse, but two kept on, wielding their sticks like swords. Midhir slipped off the horse and pulled one man away, flinging him into the hedge. The other dropped his stick and threw himself at Midhir. But as Midhir turned, knocking him down, the other rose from the hedge behind him, grabbing a branch to steady him. The bush came out of the earth to the roots. He struck Midhir on the neck, and as Midhir sank to his knees, the man rammed a branch into his eye, and twisted it, ripping his eye out of its socket.

At that moment the sky and earth were torn away from him. He was gripped by pain beyond any he had ever felt, the bear's claw in his eye socket, tearing deeper for the joy of it, past hunger, past anger, rocking him as a cat puts its claw into a mouse and plays with it past death. And there was wet, sticky blood on his face and neck, and the grass drinking it. There was no sound of fighting now, but the river lapping at the bank and his own gasping breath. He touched his face and felt his eye, crushed, soft as a turtle's egg, or a bird's when the shell doesn't form, held to the socket by shreds of muscle. And the truth came to him, sharper than the pain; that he was no longer king of Brí Léith, for no man can be king in Ireland if he is not whole.

He was carried across the ford and the field and into the Brugh. He heard Aonghus send a horseman for Dian Cecht, the physician of the Daghdha. Time passed in the dark and then Dian Cecht was there, giving him a drink that tasted of honey and poppies to make him drowsy, putting kelp into the wound. His hands were gentle, taking the eye, laying it back into the socket. He covered both eyes with a poultice of self-heal blossoms, of honey and clay dug from beneath an elder bush to ease the pain. He gave him a broth of tarragon, and called on the dragon, the one who sees, to aid him. When Dian Cecht left, saying there was nothing more he could do, it was Aonghus who stayed beside him in the Brugh, laying cloths on his eyes to cool the fire.

After many days and nights of dark Midhir's fever left him. Then he raised himself on one arm and called out to Aonghus to bring a chariot.

'I want to go home.'

'No, Midhir, you need rest. Your eyes must be covered a while longer.'

'I can lie in my own house. Get my chariot ready,' he said. He touched his face, his head; his hair was stiff with blood. 'Word moves fast of disaster,' he said, his voice shaking with rage. 'If I don't show myself at Brí Léith, how many days will pass before I lose my land? It will be joyful news that Midhir is destroyed.'

He took the wrappings off. Carefully he touched his left eye; he felt the crust of blood closing his swollen lid. 'Take me outside.'

Aonghus put his hands on his shoulders and they walked single file down the passage. 'I feel wind,' said Midhir. 'Are we near the entrance? We are; I feel the sun, and those are crows I hear. I am blind, so.'

'I swear by the gods my people swear by, nothing good shall come to me from this,' said Aonghus. 'Everything I have is yours. The grass dies under my feet; I poison the air I breathe, and blind a king,' wept Aonghus. Midhir felt the hilt of a knife in his hand. 'Kill me now. Don't leave me with nothing but shame.'

'Who's here, watching us?'

'No one. They're afraid of you.'

'They should be afraid. I won't go to Brí Léith; not yet. Now listen, Aonghus. You'll drive your finest bull and fifty cows to Dian Cecht in Uisnech, as reward. Tell him and everyone who speaks with you on the road that he has healed me well and restored my sight. Do you understand? I will stay with you for one year. You'll give me a chariot and a royal cloak and the most beautiful woman in Ireland. And the terms of compensation shall be known to all. Do you understand? To all.'

'I'll send riders today to Uisnech and to Brí Léith with the news,' said Aonghus, kissing him. 'I'll find the woman, and bring her to you. I won't fail you.'

He led Midhir back into the Brugh, and sent for his goldsmith, giving him instructions to make a royal mask for Midhir. The crown of the mask was heavy gold foil, curved in the arc of bull's horns. Over the eyes were two rayed sun-circles, pierced in the centre, and clasped by eagle's talons. The gold pieces were attached to a thick band of red-dyed oxhide which fit around the forehead. The mask was made openly, and when Bressal's servant asked if it was made for Midhir's funeral, the smith answered him, 'His wedding.' That servant stood among the crowd that watched the procession of Aonghus' prize bull and fifty cows pass the Brugh, and saw Aonghus' salute answered by Midhir standing in the entrance, his face in shadow.

Aonghus himself drove the cattle to Uisnech, riding beside the dun lead cow, and calling the dogs who circled and kept the bull from straying. He passed boys in wicker lake boats, men breaking black turf with short sickles, hunters at the cooking places beside streams, and all stopped to watch him.

Midhir stayed alone in the Brugh, and no one disturbed him. Flasks of water and wine were left under the threshold, and spits of broiled lamb, with baskets of oat cakes and cheese. One morning Midhir saw light when he felt his way to the entrance, and by evening he could make out the shapes of the standing stones that circled the Brugh.

That night it rained hard. The chamber was dim with the light of a small lamp. Midhir suddenly felt that he was not alone in the chamber. He reached for his staff and peered from his bed at the passage. A young she-wolf had come into the cave to get out of the storm. No beast had ever found the entrance of the Brugh open, for the stone was only moved away for Samhain and the winter solstice. She growled softly, claiming the den.

Midhir tossed a lambshank to her. She crouched, startled, after a moment trotted lightly to the meat and devoured it, watching him. When she had cleaned the bone she sniffed the blood-stained bandages, then she lay down with her head on the edge of the bed. From that day Midhir shared his meat with her. People said that he left the Brugh at night in the shape of a wolf, looking for the one who had gouged out his eye.

CHAPTER 5

Dun Echraide – The Fort of Horse-Rider

WHEN AONGHUS HAD DELIVERED the cattle to Dian Cecht he rode east and north, to Ailill Echraide's fort on the sea, for it was said that there was no woman as beautiful as his daughter, Étaín. Aonghus slept in the dry sand above a ridge of white shells, long, like brittle fingers, split and hollow. At dawn the waves were gold and salmon--coloured, and the air shimmered with light and the sound of horses neighing for oats. He rode up the headland to the fort.

Guards let him pass into the fort; they told him that Ailill had been called early, for one of his mares was in trouble delivering a foal. Aonghus crossed the courtyard to the stable. At the door a tall, silver-haired man nodded to him. Aonghus looked inside. A girl with dark brows and yellow hair knelt in the straw, a foal stretched across her knees. She stroked its short curled mane and breathed into its face. After a moment he struggled and stood. The mare nuzzled the foal's shoulder, and he turned to search for milk. The man gave his hand to the girl and she stood, putting her arms around him.

When they came out of the stable Aonghus stepped forward, saying, 'Midhir of Brí Léith sends his greetings to you. I am Aonghus, of the Brugh, his foster-son.'

'And I am Ailill Echraide. You are welcome. I had heard Midhir was injured in the games at Samhain,' he said, 'and that he hasn't returned to Brí Léith. No one has seen him.'

'He is my guest at Brugh na Bóinne. And his injury is healed. But he keeps to himself. He has always done so.'

'I am glad he is well.'

Aonghus stared at the girl. 'You must be Étaín, because surely you are the most beautiful woman in Ireland. I've come to take her to Midhir,' he said to Ailill, 'to be his wife. I will pay her bride price myself.'

'Leave us, Étaín,' said her father. When she had gone he asked, 'Is Fuamnach dead, then?'

Aonghus shook his head.

'While Fuamnach lived, I never thought Midhir would take another wife. But he can afford as many women as he wants. The truth is that Midhir can take Étaín from me easily in war, if he wishes. Perhaps you know that is his plan. He's too powerful to be in my debt. If he's cruel to Étaín, how shall I demand her rights?'

'I have tribute from many kings in Meath. I think I can pay your price.'

'You move quickly to bargain. It's a rare day that a mare and her foal are saved, past Samhain. Come inside and eat with me. Afterwards I'll show you the finest horses in Ireland.'

'I've seen Midhir pay a warrior's ransom for a colt out of one of your mares. My own grey stallion has the blood of your herd in him,' said Aonghus, as they crossed the courtyard.

'The sun's first strength is in the dew they graze upon. And Étaín's hand is on them from the day they are born. She has no fear of them at all. I've seen a stallion rearing under her, and she calm, telling him to relax, and down he goes. Then he follows her hands and goes where she asks him, with as light a rein as you'd put on a moth. Is there enough gold in your treasury to comfort the loss of her?'

'Midhir's need for her is great. I'll pay your price.'

They entered into the hall and sat by the fire, eating dark bread with honey and curds, discussing horses and cattle and winter weather.

Then Ailill said, 'It was strange to hear this news of Midhir. I could hardly believe it. I've seen him in battle. Great luck must be on the weapon that touches him.' He poured mead into their cups. 'And Midhir has fine horses, and the good will of the Daghdha — no small thing.' He drank, and when his cup was empty he set it down and said, 'Aonghus, now I'll tell you my price. My land is wooded and poor pasture. I'm tired of losing my best foals and calves to the Daghdha for the use of his land. When my cattle and horses graze my own land in summer and winter, and I can hold assemblies and games and build forts on the plains, then come back and ask for Étaín. Until that time I don't want to see you in my fort.'

Aonghus stood and bowed his head. 'This shall be done for you,' he said, and he left the hall with Ailill's laughter in his ears, and rode west.

Aonghus tied his horse to a hawthorn tree at the foot of Uisnech and began the climb. The sky was grey and the wind was a freezing blast; the Daghda's cattle huddled together in the low places. He walked over the hills, but couldn't find the fort. He couldn't tell what way he had come, and then it seemed that everywhere he walked the ground was soft, and wet and treacherous, and there were no cattle. He ran up a hall, calling out 'Father, Father,' and when he reached the top, he saw the Daghdha in his stone chair beside the ash tree.

'I made Elcmhar angry,' said Aonghus, out of breath. 'For my sake Midhir was hurt. It's his right to ask compensation. I must give him Étaín, the daughter of Ailill Echraide. But what her father asks is impossible; I have no power to pay his price, the clearing of his forests. I will fail, and you, my father, must go to war against him to fulfill Midhir's demand.'

'It's not for his own eyes that he wants beautiful Étaín,' said the Daghdha, 'but to keep his land. Étaín will give no pleasure to Fuamnach. Let Midhir have Étaín if he thinks she'll help him hold Brí Léith, but Aonghus, son of Bóinn, there's no need to go to war.' He broke a branch from the ash and began stripping off the bark. 'Go back to the Horse-Rider now.'

Before night came a storm passed Aonghus, moving east. The air had a bitter scent, and lightning struck close by. His horse shied and they took shelter in a thicket of blackthorn.

That evening, when Ailill Echraide walked along the rath he saw deer were stripping bark off the young trees at the edge of the woods. He counted more than eighty deer girdling the trees. Thunder came out of the west, and he went into his house.

But inside the woods, animals woke early from their winter sleep, and sharp hunger gripped them, so that their drowsiness left them. Red squirrels, badgers and stoats grew ravenous and began to strip the trees. Bears sharpened their claws on ash, shredding the diamond bark. Boars rubbed their tusks against oaks. Pine needles turned red and dropped to the forest floor. The wind grew strong. The last oak leaves fell; all the trees were dead and bare.

On the hill of Uisnech the Daghdha laid his double headed axe to an oak whose girth could hide a horse, and split it to the ground. Then lightning struck the woods of Ailill Echraide, struck a hundred times in one beat of the bodhran. Trees exploded into flame. In the fields horses screamed and ran. Leaves and needles kindled fires that swept the trees from the land of Ailill Echraide into the sky.

When morning came the wind was dark with ash. Ailill carried water to the horses from a running stream, for every still pond was black with cinders. As he walked over his land to see that all his horses were well, it began to rain. When the clouds drifted off over the sea, and the sun was bright, he saw new grass on the burnt ground.

That day Aonghus stood before the gate of the fort, and said, 'I have cleared the plains of Mag Machae, Mag Lemna, Mag nItha, Mag Tochair, Mag nDula, Mag Techt, Mag Li, Mag Line and Mag Muithemni. Now give me Étaín, and I will take her to the Brugh where Midhir waits for her.'

'What does the Daghdha owe to Midhir the Proud, and to young Aonghus, that he'll show his power so freely?' asked Ailill. 'Who will succeed him at Uisnech? He'll stay forever on that hill, with his stone and his tree, and the tribute of the whole island coming to him, though others starve.

'You will not have her until my bogs are drained so that rivers flow across my land to the sea. When my people can grow corn in their fields, and fish to stop their hunger, then, rich Aonghus of the Brugh, come talk to me about Étaín.'

When Aonghus stood on the hill of Uisnech and called the Daghdha, his father came, and he told him what Ailill had demanded. 'Now I'm ready to go to war against Ailill Echraide, who has no respect for the Lord of Uisnech. Will you help me?'

The Daghdha said nothing. Aonghus followed him to a small pond, circled by stones and thick grass. Blue dragonflies skimmed the surface. The pool was deep; Aonghus couldn't see the bottom. 'Aonghus, my son, see how his eye is dark,' the Daghdha said softly. 'He's sleeping.'

'Nathrach, serpent of three eyelids, wake.' He stepped to the edge. His reflection filled the pool. 'Now you see me. Are you hungry?' He touched the sweat on his forehead, then put his hand in the pool. 'Nathrach; taste the salt of my blood. Drowsy you lie under your blanket of earth and grass, waiting for something small to stumble at the pond's edge. This day a mole or frog, the next a duckling. But your hunger grows.

'In the east, where the water tastes of blood, salt of living food, tossed on the moon's arm, the current brings fish, quick salmon that leap to your mouth, and things that crunch: crabs and slow things that move along the bottom, always in reach. Stir, now, Nathrach, with your long tongue, and find the sea.'

The Daghdha dried his hands on the grass, took up his bodhran and began to play. First he moved his left hand inside the drum across the skin, muting the sound. Then he let the sound grow, louder and deeper and faster until the drumming became one single liquid sound that Aonghus could no longer hear, but felt in his chest, in his arms and hands.

Beetles and ants came out of the earth. A badger and her young crawled out of their burrow into the open. Cattle lay down in the pastures; the crows left the trees. A dog howled.

From the ground came a sound like a thousand horses running, and the earth shook. The water in the pond broke in waves. Fish came dead to the surface. The earth moved like water. Trees swayed and fell.

In the east lakes and wells shuddered, and from them great cracks opened in the earth, and ran east. Where the land opened, the water that lay under the ground and above the ground filled the cracks and flowed to the sea. And the new rivers were called Blackwater, Mourne, Slenae, Nass, Amnas, Oichen, Or, Bann, Samuir and Lochae; and salmon found their way into them.

That night the earth grew quieter, with only trembling that comes and goes like a child who sleeps worn from crying.

But when Aonghus reached Ailill's gate, he was refused again. 'I won't give my daughter to you,' said Ailill. 'Everything you've done has been for her people, but I myself will have no further good of her. How can I make up her loss?'

'What do you want for her, then?' asked Aonghus.

'I want her weight in gold and silver,' he said, 'and that will be my share in her price.'

'It will be done,' answered Aonghus. When he reached the Brugh he collected all the gold and silver ingots in his hoard, the wealth of tribute he had taken that year as Lord of the Brugh, and he put them in sacks and loaded them on a cart with solid oak wheels. He drove north again, with the cart and twenty warriors following. And when he reached the fort, the gates opened for him, and Ailill walked solemnly beside him into the house.

CHAPTER 6

The Long Night

ÉTAÍN HORSE-RIDER WAITED in the hall beside the scales that her father used to measure out grain for his horses. Her father and Aonghus with dark hair and grey eyes came in together, then Aonghus stood aside while her father gave orders to the servants carrying small, heavy sacks to the scales. When she laid her cloak on the floor and stepped naked into the scales, he stood with his back to her, adding gold and silver ingots until her father said, 'Enough!' and she stepped down, and covered herself again.

The two men spit into their hands and touched palms, making their bargain fast. Then Aonghus looked at her, and he said, 'Your honour price is my own; and I swear that if anyone harms you, their life or mine will be forfeit.' Her father nodded and left the hall.

Aonghus rode beside her out of the fort, with his guards coming behind, leading her horses. At the river, Étaín kicked her stallion and he bolted. She looked back and saw Aonghus following, his stallion flying over the field. She gave the reins and her horse ran faster; when the land rose she reined him. Aonghus caught her, and they fell out of a gallop, their horses' chests and legs and jaws white with lather. He looked at her, out of breath, and she saw his fear.

'Did you think I'd broken the bargain? So much gold and nothing to bring home to Midhir? I wasn't going to run away,' she laughed. 'I love Midhir of Brí Léith.'

'You know him, then?'

'I do.'

His eyes were grave; he took her rein. They walked, crossing meadows brilliant with new grass. 'Look how the heartsease has blossomed again from the fire.'

'The Daghdha has given a second summer for your wedding.' They stopped to rest the horses, and he wove a basket of reeds and she filled it with violets and cowslip, dogrose and blue gentian.

'Tell me about the Brugh, where you live,' she said.

'There's a house beside the mound with room for a hundred chieftains. A stable for twenty stallions, and the byre. The river lies below like a torc,' he said, lightly tracing the curve of her gold necklace with his fingers. He didn't look up, and Étaín saw that the shape of his brows was like Midhir's, two narrow black feathers. She stroked his eyebrow lightly with the back of one finger. He looked up at her, his grey eyes grave, and she smiled.

Aonghus stood up. 'There are swans on the river; sometimes a hundred of them in winter. Standing stones circle the mound of the Brugh; like white horses grazing day and night, never moving. And when the sky is clear at dawn, mid-winter, the Brugh is filled with light. There are voices in the stones.' He stopped and looked down at her.

'I will see these things for myself, and know that they're true. You've told them well. But I've seen the stones move in the moonlight, and shake their manes at a sound, or the wind. In my dreams I've stood on Brí Léith, the mountain of crystal.'

They heard the heavy carts coming; Aonghus gave her his hand, and pulled her standing.

That night they camped beside the river Boyne. Aonghus and Étaín made a bed of rushes and blankets on a hill, with her stallion tethered, and the mares grazing around them. They watched the mist come over the hills, turning them violet; the green pasture brightening under the mist, then fading as the mist came in, lying close to the river, and the sky grew dark.

Étaín unbraided her hair, and shook it out. Aonghus watched her, carving an alder twig, then blowing a tuneless song from the green pipe.

'How far is it now?' she asked.

Aonghus put the pipe down in the grass. 'An easy ride tomorrow. I've sent a rider ahead. We don't need to reach the Brugh before dark. Sleep long if you like.'

She lay down, her hair spread out around her on the grass, and shut her eyes. 'I can't sleep at all,' she said, laughing, and sat up, throwing a handful of rushes at him.

He caught her hand and she leaned against him, her head on his shoulder.

'I'm in love with you,' he said.

Étaín was silent.

'I could keep you for my own,' he said.

'You could easily,' she said, and closed her eyes, not moving. The wind rose up. When she opened her eyes the mist was nearly gone from the river, and she could see the waves, white-ridged from the wind.

'Aonghus.' She felt his breath warm on her face. 'There's no harm in you,' she said to him. He didn't answer. She lay back against the hill, and he beside her, a little apart. After awhile the sky cleared, and they named all the stars they knew.

The next day they followed the river to the Brugh. Guards met them at dusk and gave them escort. There were torches around the mound and beside a tent of painted oxhide near the river where Étaín went alone to prepare herself.

Inside the chamber, Midhir put on the royal cloak that Aonghus had given him, and the gold mask, with talons clasping the eyeholes. At the entrance he heard the creak of chariot wheels coming towards him. There was a long blur of torches below. The chariot stopped behind the entrance stone. Two people stepped out. Then Aonghus touched his arm, and put a woman's hand in his, and Midhir followed her into the passage.

The woman put his hand on her cool cheek. 'Midhir,' she said, and he knew her voice. Then her mouth was on his mouth, and she kissed him with a binding kiss that went straight to his chest, that fused him heart to heart, sinew to sinew, even while he stood astonished, with the feel of her lips on his still. He heard her ask, 'Midhir, how are you wounded?' and she unfastened the mask from his forehead, her arms stretched up to reach the clasp behind his head, the soft wool of her cloak against his face. 'My stallion is in your stable, Midhir,' she said. 'Let me see your eyes.' He let her touch his face, not moving. Then she went away and he heard her pouring water into a basin. She held a cup to his lips and he drank. She dipped the edge of her dress into the water and laid it against his eyes.

Under the dark lid the torn places of the eye began to grow and mend, and the eye itself filled with fluid. At the edges of the socket shreds of muscle stretched and grasped the eye. And behind the full, white shining orb, the fine tendrils of sight reached out, spreading, sparkling into the centre dark and the talons that grasped the edge of blue let go and Midhir could see.

He saw the basin quiver and come clear, rings spreading from the tiny drops that fell from his face into the water, and then as the surface stilled, in the bottom of the basin, two stones of sapphire. Then he saw that the stones were his own eyes, reflected, healed. He looked up and saw Étaín.

As white as the snow of a single night were her wrists, pure white and tapering her fingers. She unbraided her hair, two braids of four locks with a small globe of gold at the end. She shook out her mane of gold; it fell past her waist. Her hair was like burnished red gold, as black as a beetle's back were her brows. Her eyes were lapis blue; her lips red as foxglove. He met her eyes, and walked the bridge of the sword's edge. He said, 'Lovely anyone until Étaín. Beautiful anyone until Étaín.' He watched her smooth her hair with a silver comb. She unfastened the brooch that closed her soft, curly crimson fleece cloak. Her long-hooded tunic was of stiff silk, green as the grass with the winter light in it, embroidered with red-gold beasts at her breasts and her shoulders. She let it fall to the ground, and bathed her arms from the basin.

Her shoulders were straight, smooth and soft; as white as seafoam her side, slender, long, smooth and yielding. Warm and smooth, sleek and white her thighs; round and small, firm and white her knees. Fine and straight were her heels; she had the walk of a queen.

She laughed, and it was the voice Midhir remembered, the child's laugh of joy when her horse reared, and she was astride. When she laughed the Brugh came back, and great white swans roosting above the corbelled ceiling of the chamber, their nest the wide mound of the Brugh, shook their long wings and their feathers shimmered down over the standing stones. The moon basins rose above the floor, pulling the tide across the stone, breaking and falling with a hush.

Midhir covered her with his robe, and looked at her long before he touched her skin. He put his hands in her hair and then sorrow pierced him, that the moment would pass from him, that he might not keep her. He thought, 'Now I have become dangerous, and I must welcome what comes, if it be the destruction of the world, to keep her.' He touched her skin, and kissed her throat, the blossoms of her white breasts, and he said, '*Bé Find*, my pale woman, my Étaín, you must not stray from me now.' Then he made love to her, and there was peace between them.

That night was the longest night of the year, and when they woke the lamps had gone out, and the dark was complete. They held each other talking softly. And soon after dawn the floor of the chamber began to glow, and the stones along the wall burned hearth red. The spirals turned; vapour rose from the basin up into the luminous turning roof. Wind moved through the chamber and there were voices in it, voices in the chiselled spirals and up in the chamber ceiling; and the human ribs carved in the side of the pillar stone breathed.

Midhir whispered, holding Étaín, 'Even the bones of earth are brought alive.' And he sang,

'Wake now, from your cold sleep.
You live forever.
Remember the day of your making.
The first morning is come again.
The sun's red forge burns again in the mountain.

Now the kingfisher flies from the sun,
His feet red with fire;
Hunger on him,
He breaks the river
Spears fish in air.
Rain pours down,
Grain flows from the living stone.
Vines climb,
Petals open,
The ram's horn curls,
Here on the tips of your fingers.'

He kissed her hands, and then he took her in one motion
down on his bed, and he loved her. And when the chamber
was dark again, and they lay still, Étaín leaned over him,
and kissed his eyes. Then they dressed and went outside to
show themselves to the people of the Brugh.

CHAPTER 7

The Boar Hunt

ONE EVENING NEAR SUMMER'S END Midhir and Étaín took a young mare to the field above the Brugh. Weeks of rain had left the river swollen, and the pastures beside the river were too soft for working horses. He watched her hook a long rope through the ring attached to the halter, up behind the mare's ears and over her head through the other side. She let out the rope from loops gathered in one hand, in the other she held a whip, and lightly flicked it behind the mare's hind legs. The horse bolted and Étaín followed her a few steps, letting the rope go taut. The mare slowed, breaking into a trot, and Étaín turned sunwise, letting out the rope, lengthening the circle, keeping the long whip poised at her flanks. The mare's head was up, her coat was wet and shining. Étaín talked to her, watching her movement, keeping her moving out at a fast trot, then a canter. Gradually the mare's head came down and her stride lengthened, bending as Étaín drew the rope in and the circle tighter. There was a distant crack of thunder.

'Storm's coming,' said Aonghus, walking up beside him. 'Better go in.' He nodded toward Étaín.

'That mare's moving well today,' said Midhir. 'Good bone and balance. Étaín wants to ride her to Brí Léith; she'll be ready.'

Aonghus said, 'Why must you go?'

'Because Brí Léith is my kingdom, and Étaín belongs to me, not you.'

'You forget Fuamnach.'

'You forget yourself, boy.'

'We are the same age, Étaín and I.'

Midhir stopped Étaín, taking the mare's lead rope.

'What's wrong?' she asked Midhir. He didn't answer. She looked at Aonghus. 'I heard thunder,' he said.

Midhir put his arm around Étaín and they walked down to the stable. When they'd fed the mare Aonghus came in, his hair streaming with rain.

That night it rained without stopping. Étaín quietly left Midhir's bed in the house below the Brugh. She ran in the hard rain to the top of the mound; in a stroke of lightning she saw that the river had come over its banks, and was spreading fast across the plain of the Brugh. She saw the current in it, taking branches and felled trees. Her mares and foals were out on the fields beside the river. She ran to the stable. There was light inside, and Aonghus's dogs leapt on her at the door. 'Aonghus! Did you see the river?'

'I'm going to bring them in,' he answered from the end of the passageway, bringing his stallion around. 'Go on back.'

She slid a jointed bit up into her stallion's mouth, laid her right palm flat on his back and swung herself up onto him.

They rode out into the rain, descending slowly towards the edge of the dark, fast-moving water. In flashes of lightning Étaín saw whole trees floating past, a curragh spinning, and a cart wheel, its spokes sticking up like spears in a corpse. The torrent was loud above the rain and thunder. The mares' eyes gleamed in the dark ahead. Their stallions neighed and the mares answered.

'There's high water between us,' cried Étaín.

'Stay back,' Aonghus yelled and he rode forward. then turned and cantered back. 'That stream's deep and rising but not fast. They can cross it if we take them now, before it joins the river.'

Étaín sent her stallion forward. Lightning cracked; she saw black water just under her feet. The stallion slipped and stumbled and she lost the reins. She grabbed his mane and pressed him hard; she felt him gathering, coming under, then they burst into a gallop as he found footing and pulled out of the water. Aonghus was beside her; he caught her reins. They gathered the mares and foals, then drove them into the water, and out again onto high ground.

For the rest of the night Étaín and Aonghus watched, walking their stallions through the herd. The rain let up. Near dawn the clouds passed away. The river found its high mark and began to fall.

At daybreak they started home. Mud clung to stalks and weeds in the pasture. On the far shore of the Boyne the woods stood in water. The foals streaked around standing pools, around a mass of down and river grass, the remains of a swan's nest. They came to the body of a drowned colt. Étaín slipped down from her horse, and knelt beside the foal. She stroked his neck, ran her hand through the short soft mane, wind-dried, cleared the mud from his eyes.

'Now they are coming, I hear them.
Horses of many colours, coming,
From the west they are coming.

White horses at the river,
I hear their crossing.
Now they go east,
On the white road.
Together we go now,
On the white road.'

When Étaín looked up Aonghus was slowly threading his stallion through the herd. Behind him rose the mound of the Brugh. Aonghus halted his horse when she reached him, waited for her to speak. 'Midhir's waiting,' she said. 'I'm going ahead.' She galloped to the stable.

Midhir took her horse when she came in. She wiped mud from her face and arms with a cloth, ashamed that he would see her so filthy; but he didn't look at her.

'I thought there were two horses stolen last night, but here is one returning,' he said to himself, brushing the stallion. 'Here's a mystery: one stall remains empty. If I find who has taken the stallion, they shall die for it. He belonged to me once, and he's very valuable.'

'I lost only one colt; we were lucky. Your property's safe, Midhir.'

'It will be soon,' he said, holding the horse's front foot in his hand, the cleaning hook in the other.

She went to him and put her hand on his arm. 'I couldn't sleep. I heard the storm. I didn't wake Aonghus; he was out in it; he was the river too,' she said. 'We moved the horses to high ground, then we couldn't get back.'

'You can see in the dark, Étaín.'

'I cannot.'

'You're afraid of nothing.'

Her voice was low. 'It would be a terrible thing, to drown. Maybe I don't know you.'

She walked out of the stall; he followed and put his arms around her. 'You're cold,' he said. 'Your clothes are soaked.'

'Midhir, forgive me; I should have waked you–' she said, kissing him.

He held her face in his hands, looking into her eyes. 'Beautiful Étaín,' he said, and kissed her.

'Forgive me,' she murmured.

'Hush...you're so tired.' He took off her wet clothes and wrapped his cloak around her, then picked her up in his arms, and carried her into the house, to her bed, like a child.

That night Midhir ordered a feast because the mares and the foals were saved. Aonghus sat on his left and Étaín on his right as they had always done. Down the length of the table one hundred candles burned. There were spits of roast lamb with leeks and garlic, and small pies of goat cheese and fennel, the crust laced with onions and butter. There was venison stew, and cold salmon and trout. There were sweet apples in thick cream on cakes made of eggs and ground hazelnuts, oatcakes with pears, pitchers of foaming ale, and a cask of dark wine from the land south beyond the sea.

When they had drunk the health of the company, Midhir filled his glass again and said, 'Tomorrow night let there be roast boar on this table, and a drinking horn for Aonghus of the boar's tusk.'

A shout of pleasure answered him from the long table, and a drumming of fists. 'The river has flooded the boar's den,' said Midhir, 'and drowned the woods. The dogs will flush him out easily. Aonghus has never hunted boar; he was young at Brí Léith, but now he's Lord of the Brugh, and a man. He'll ride with me, tomorrow at dawn.' He put his hand on Aonghus' shoulder. 'Who rides with us?' cried Midhir. Every man's glass was raised to his. Aonghus beside him nodded, his eyes shining. The pitchers were filled again, and cups raised, and soon the pipes and the flute were drowned by the talk of the hunt, of weapons and dogs.

Étaín got up from the table. Midhir saw that she hadn't touched her food or the drink beside the plate. He watched her walk the length of the table, her tunic swirling below her hips like the tide, the white silk heavy with amber beads sewn in spirals from the waist to the hem. She walked between the two guards at the hall door, with the spears of the company laid out on either side of the threshold, and as she passed, one of the guards whispered and the other laughed. Midhir knew that every person in the hall heard him, for they had gone silent as Étaín passed, with her hair and the amber of her dress catching the candle light, like furze in summer when the sun comes suddenly out from a cloud.

The man said, 'I don't know who Étaín will sleep with tonight, but I know that beautiful Étaín won't sleep alone.'

Midhir said to his guards behind him, 'Take them out and hang them. Don't let the edge of a sword touch them, for they foul the metals of earth.' To Aonghus he said, 'See that you sleep before the night is done; a night of too much wine and too little sleep may dull your aim when the boar turns and finds you.' Then he bowed to the company and went out of the hall.

There was frost on the ground the next morning, and ice in the troughs. The horses were given extra grain, and bowls of steaming water were poured into their troughs. The riders wore heavy sheepskin capes, and boots and gloves of leather lined with fur, and carried flasks of liquor. The reeds at the river's edge were silver pipes sprouting from the frozen ground. The hunters crossed the ford, snapping the ice under their horses' hooves, the big dogs circling and drinking from the broken puddles, then moving back to their master's calls.

They rode slowly into the oak wood, looking for tracks, following the bend of the river and the rising ground. The sun came up, turning the east sides of the trees to gold, casting shafts of gold, like spears, between them. The rowan and hazel and oaks began to diminish, and yews and pines increase, and the forest got darker. Suddenly the dogs cried and ran ahead. Their cries became faint and then stopped. After a while those who had lost the scent came back. The men rode on, ducking under branches, following the rough deer trail the dogs had taken.

They rode into a bend of the path, and Midhir raised his arm in a signal to halt. There was a rustling sound ahead, out of view. They went forward slowly until they could see straight into the woods for twenty paces or more, and there in the middle of the path, under the roof of cedars, some living thing flip-flopped upon the leaves. Legs and torso flailed in aimless jerks. It made no cry; there was only the sound of its body hitting the damp leaves. Midhir rode forward and speared the animal, and its spasm ceased. The dog lay still in death, its back broken by the boar's tusk.

They rode on. The woods were still; no birds stirred or sang. The ground led down, where trees still stood in water. The dogs splashed through the thin sheet of ice that covered the brackish water where the sun had not touched it, moving back and forth before the horses, sniffing the air and the trees.

Someone's horse balked and refused to go forward; another shied. 'The horses don't like it here,' said Midhir, 'and the dogs are no use in all this water. Go back to the rise where the ground is dry. We'll hear the dogs if you see him. Come, Aonghus, with me. We'll go on farther here.'

The rest of the hunters turned their horses and went back.

'He's close by; he's watching us,' said Midhir quietly as they rode on.

'You can't take Étaín to Brí Léith,' said Aonghus suddenly.

'I can't? Shall I leave her here, instead, with you?'

'Fuamnach will kill her. I swore to keep her safe.'

'Don't think about Étaín, Aonghus. Think about the boar, and your horse, and where you'll put your blade. Your bow is useless, Aonghus. His skin is a shield, harder than copper, harder than bronze. Arrows fall from it as they fall from a stone. What will you use, Aonghus, when he charges, and opens your horse's chest with his tusks, and you fall together, and his tusk is there, somewhere, rooting and seeking; and it takes only one thrust to kill you, but he's fast and can give many thrusts; and you have one chance to kill him, only one?'

'Then stay here, with her, Midhir, or send her to Uisnech, but don't – '

'Be careful! I see your hunger.' He turned his horse and looked around him. Their horses stood in water past the fetlocks, trembling. Bare thorned twigs, blackthorn, roses and blackberries stuck out of the water. The sun was a weak yellow orb through the drooping branches of the cedars; under it a small hill rose from the water, covered with hazel and oak saplings. Aonghus's three dogs leapt from the water onto the dry ground, sniffing the edge of the hazel thicket. Then they stopped, and crouched, growling, their teeth bared.

Midhir and Aonghus rode up the hill. Then they could see the boar behind the thicket, watching them. His hard-muscled neck was as broad as a man's shoulders, with a stiff high ridge along his back, like the blade of a sickle.

Aonghus moved slowly. He fixed a spear point on the shaft and raised his arm. Then the boar came out. The spear flew at the same moment the boar charged the dogs. There was a blur, and the dogs in a huddle, screaming, and a violent shudder at the edge of the blur as the boar stopped hard. In a breath his tusk came out of the dog's shoulder bright and dripping, and Aonghus's spear bounced and lay flat on the ground.

He held a second spear high as his horse wheeled and reared. He hurled it hard and it caught the boar above his back leg and held. The boar charged the horse, dragging the spear. Aonghus's horse turned and kicked frantically, his legs curved as the boar kept under him, nodding and stabbing. Then Aonghus lost his sword, pulled from his horse. He was on the ground, and the boar was trampling him.

Midhir whipped Aonghus's horse across the breast and he jumped to the side. He flung a spear straight down and pierced the boar's back. As he slid down from his own horse the boar left Aonghus and charged. Midhir drove his sword into his chest up to the hilt.

The boar collapsed onto its side at the edge of the water, biting furiously at the sword, dark blood spreading around him. Then he weakened and fell back, came up again, relaxed, and sank at last into the water.

Midhir helped Aonghus to stand, and saw that his wounds were not deep. 'You did well not to move,' he said to Aonghus. 'He couldn't get his tusks under you.' He walked into the icy, brackish water, put his foot against the boar's chest and pulled out his sword.

'His eyes are so small,' said Aonghus, his teeth chattering.

'I wouldn't have thought that,' said Midhir, quietly, 'not so small. Tomorrow Étaín and I go to Brí Léith.' He saw Aonghus's look, but the boy said nothing to him, turning away to examine his horse's bleeding legs. He walked the horse into the cold standing water to close the wounds, and Midhir blew three notes on the bronze horn, to call the hunters in. When they came they marvelled at the size of the tusks and the polished whiteness of them. They cut off the boar's head, and Midhir's lackey carried it behind him, and laid the carcass out on a pole to take it back to the Brugh.

When Étaín met him at the door of the great hall, food and wine waiting for them, he told her that they wouldn't wait any longer, but that she must make preparations that night, for they would leave the Brugh at first light.

CHAPTER 1

Brí Léith – The Rowan Wand

THE MOUNTAIN WAS COVERED with fog when Midhir's royal procession started up the winding path to Brí Léith. A soft rain fell on them, on Midhir's black cloak that covered his tunic of linked crescents, made of shaved horses' hooves. It fell on the gold mass of Étaín's hair, on her purple robe dyed of dogwhelk shell, with a thousand lapis beads at the neck and sleeves, and on her white stallion with his mane braided, looped and tied with gold.

The track was narrow and steep; they went single file, stopping as guards moved rocks and branches from the path. 'In summer you'll swear foxglove grows from every stone beside the road,' said Midhir to Étaín. The forest was blurred beyond the brown ferns; but as they neared the top of the mountain they came out of the mist, and Étaín could see the plains far below. Up ahead people stood on the path, their cloaks moving in the wind.

She rode beside Midhir along the quartz rampart of the fort that circled the mound and Midhir's house on it shining like a rock silver and wet from the sea. Guards herded children back from the chariot wheels and the horses as they entered the fort, and the people stared at her. They halted before his house.

There was a woman waiting on the steps, surrounded by guards. Her red hair was plaited and coiled around her head. Her eyelids were painted gold; she wore a green dress of heavy silk, and a cape of green-dyed swan's down. The wind lifted feathers at her shoulders, but she stood very still, her hands folded over a stick of rowan.

Midhir dismounted, took her hand and kissed her lightly. 'You have kept Brí Léith well for me, Fuamnach. I'm grateful,' and he took the gold torc from his neck, and put it on her. 'This is Étaín Echraide, a stranger to Brí Leith, who healed me when I was injured in the games. Fuamnach, you must teach the people to show her honour. Now, Étaín, you'll see your horses settled.'

They went to the stables, and the woman Fuamnach came with them. She stopped the boy carrying hay to the stall, and pulled the bundle apart, looking for black rot or poisonous grey dust. 'It's fresh, this summer's harvest,' said Fuamnach, but he was showing Étaín a white colt and didn't seem to hear her.

Fuamnach followed them to the blacksmith's house, and showed them what had been made that year, the weapons, bridles and cauldrons of bronze; and to the wheelwright's, where they saw new chariots and carts. Everywhere they went Midhir walked beside Étaín; and he too looked at her, as the people stared.

They drove two chariots out to the fields where the cattle and sheep grazed. They walked over the land, and Midhir showed Étaín the pastures, the woods and the plains below. Fuamnach told the numbers of the new calves and lambs and stories of animals they both knew. He took Étaín's hand and smiled at her. 'it's good to see you walk on my fields,' he said.

When they returned to the chariots, he said, 'You must be tired, Étaín. We'll go in now and you'll sleep.' He turned his chariot toward the house.

Fuamnach raised the whip in her hand, and stopped his horse.

'Étaín must come first to my house,' she said. 'I want to show her the glade of healing herbs, and the stream where the goldsmith cools his forge that flows by my house. The water is sweet from that stream. There is a berry that I have found that gives refreshing sleep after a hard ride.' She looked at Étaín. 'You must not shame me by refusing to drink with me.'

'I'll come with you, and gladly, Fuamnach.'

Midhir said, 'Fuamnach's found herbs that grow only on this mountain and many others you wouldn't see in the east. I'll wait for you in the house. Tonight you won't eat traveller's bread; there'll be a feast.'

Fuamnach gave Étaín her hand into her chariot, and she turned the horses toward the pine forest.

They crossed the rocky stream lined with cress, nettles and ferns, and ducked under a large rowan tree that stood beside the door of the small wood and wattle house. There was one dark room. A single, carved chair stood before the hearth.

'The house is cold,' said Fuamnach. 'Wait here while I get kindling for the fire.'

She laid her rowan whip against the door and went out of the house. Étaín sat down in the chair. There were bundles of dried herbs hanging from the beams. A pine marten ran along the beam and disappeared into a hole in the thatch. There was no furniture in the one room except the chair, not a blanket or a shawl or piece of crockery. The earthen floor was swept clean. There was one window facing the stream, and a branch of the rowan heavy with red berries hung over the sill.

Fuamnach came in through the door, her arms full of branches. She put them into the hearth. Then she stood in front of Étaín, placing her hand on Étaín's shoulder. 'You've taken the chair of a good woman,' she said.

She struck her with the rowan whip. 'Horse-rider, you will obey me.'

Then everything began to change. Étaín saw Fuamnach's green eyes blur, then her face, and the room. It was as if she herself were under water. She could not gasp to take a breath, she couldn't move; she could hear Fuamnach's voice muted and distant.

'Scream, Étaín. Your stallion won't answer? I gave him a feast of laurel leaves. He dies, Étaín, he dies for you, for your love. You can't strike me now with your sharp hooves, Horse-rider. They are hidden still. You will never use them. Did you think Midhir would lie between us?'

She came closer. Étaín could not breathe; pain filled her chest, the room. Slowly Fuamnach knelt before her chair, and words crooned to Étaín's ear:

'I see him with your eyes, I touch him with your hands. Beautiful Étaín, we are one. But I breathe and drink. You are a mere reflection only. Rowan, quicken tree, find water. Drench what burns. Let what was water become water again. Let blood return to the earth. All things turn back to water. Flesh and blood. Stone and stream. Spirit of water. Break! Be gone.'

When she touched Étaín's cheek, Fuamnach's face and shoulders and the room behind her burst into fragments, and then Étaín saw nothing.

Fuamnach stood alone in the room. Water spread slowly across the floor. Rings grew out from the empty chair. She left the house. She caught the two horses that she had left grazing in the small meadow behind her house, and harnessed them to her chariot. She drove through the fortress gates down the mountain, east, towards Dowth.

When Midhir woke from his sleep he saw that it was getting dark and Étaín had not returned. He wrapped a cloak around him, took his staff and went out of the house. He began calling Étaín when he reached the woods. The door of Fuamnach's house was standing open. He went in. The house was empty and dark, and the floor was covered with water. He went outside and walked along the stream. The level of the water was close to the bank, although it had not rained while he slept. In the wet ground beside the stream he found the marks of hooves and chariot wheels going into the woods. He ran through the forest calling Étaín, and as he ran, around him the hidden spaces under the fir trees, the caves and burrows were lit up, but he could find no trace of her.

When he reached the stable he heard voices; there was a commotion at the door. The stable servants were running in with buckets of steaming water, and Midhir's groom was yelling instructions. His stallion and Étaín's were down in their stalls, groaning and soaked with sweat. The signs were clear: he saw the poisonous dry laurel leaves in their stalls; they would not recover. Fuamnach's chariot and horses were gone. His guards had seen her drive alone through the gate.

Midhir went back into the woods, and he lay down on the wet ground, and pressed holly against his face. He lay in the leaves until the cold numbed him and it was dark. From that night, Fuamnach's house was left to the water and the woods, and Midhir gave orders that no one should go near it.

Snow came early that winter and it lasted. Wolves ranged out of their territories and cattle and sheep froze in the fields. That winter Midhir hunted boar, and when there were no boar left in his forests, then he went to war. With his thousand warriors on their heavy coated warhorses, Midhir drove off his enemies. From Brí Léith to the wide Shannon River chieftains despaired, their young men killed and their animals slaughtered. When their children cried for hunger, they gave up their land and weapons to Midhir and he sent them grain.

Ice formed on the pool in Fuamnach's house, and owls nested in the slanting beams. The rough-skinned berries ripened on the caithne tree. Midhir did not go there, except when he passed it on his way to war, and a thousand horses left the imprint of their hooves in the snow beside the stream. He never talked of Étaín, but those of his warriors who had seen her spoke privately of her bright hair and her red mouth, and how no woman was her equal for beauty. Midhir took no women slaves for his own use.

Ravens watched and followed him, and ate the eyes of the dead on the battlefield. People said that the birds spoke to Midhir, and that if Midhir looked a man in the face, that man could tell by his eyes if he would live or die.

One night Midhir lay outside among his sleeping warriors waiting for dawn and the hour of attack. He saw a patch of dark like a spearhead coming out of the south, blotting out the stars. As the shape passed overhead, it swerved and caught the moonlight. They were swans, flying low in one form and motion as if they were chained together. The night was warm. Midhir threw off his sheepskin cape, and got up, watching them until they disappeared over the trees in the north.

When he returned to Brí Léith, he went to the house in the woods. There were cracks in the earth around the pool, green sprouts coming up, yellow five-pointed blossoms at the edge of the pond, and the white draighean flower open on the blackthorn. Azure dragonflies skimmed the pool and drank at its edge, and an emerald green worm moved slowly along a branch of a young birch tree beside the pool. A wren made her nest in the thatch. The next day he put his weapons and his armour aside and he sent his warriors to the fields with seed, and to tend the new lambs and calves.

At Bealtaine he poured fresh milk into the carved cups in the stones of the cairn on Brí Léith, and he made a bonfire that was seen on the hill of Uisnech and the shores of the Cold Lake. Ash from the bones of the slain animals was planted with the new seed, and the ribs of Midhir's cattle and horses vanished under their sleek hides as the new summer grass came thick and rich.

When the leaves were full on the oak and rowan, he went again to the house in the woods. The pool was nearly gone. On an oak tree a huge purple butterfly unfurled its wings from a green silken cocoon. Its dark, luminous wings were wet, and it moved them slowly and with great effort, like an animal panting with exhaustion. When the wings were dry the butterfly opened them wide. There was a dark eye in each wing. It flew down to the edge of the pool to drink. For one moment, before the butterfly touched the water and broke the reflection, Midhir saw Étaín in her green silk tunic and her cloak of purple fleece.

He stood perfectly still. After a time the butterfly flew to his shoulder and settled there. As dusk came on he walked with her on his cloak. He saw new ferns uncoil and the knots in the joints of oaks, the diamond bark of the ash. He saw below the bark, the slow spinning rings. The pattern of veins in an oak leaf was the shape of its branches, and the mountain, and the river feathering the plain below, and the veins of Étaín's wings.

'Now we know each other's minds.

Raven, wolf and boar; but hunters, hunted.
How wise they are to hide desire;
How foolish I to have forgotten.
Too late now to turn away,
I see the fast pulse in your throat
And my sweat stains the air.

There is no home but hiding place:
Moss, water, leaves, holes.
The serpent is here; she takes
Fern, flower, boar and buck,
Close in her coil to stall hunger.
Breath is spasm only.

Now it comes hard,
I must remember to draw air.
My name is lost, my father's face,

The shape of my land.
Make an end of this motion.
Death is sweet, still and dark.'

The forest grew cold; Étaín's wings closed, her eyes hidden. The sun was going down. A mass of cloudfire turned and stretched across the sky. The fire spread to the trees and grass and the scarlet of her wings. Midhir looked at the palms of his hands; they were luminous. He saw the blood move in veins under the skin. A badger came out of a hedge and stared at him. Midhir knew his thought, and what he and the beast would do.

CHAPTER 2

Dowth – The Dark Hill

IN DOWTH, FUAMNACH SAT before the fire, drinking a sweet summer wine made from elder blossoms. Bressal watched her from across the dark room. That night he had given her a robe of violet silk, that showed her white neck and her breasts, and held the firelight. She pushed up the gold bracelets on her arms, and stirred the coals.

'They say that Midhir has not taken another woman.'

Bressal laughed. 'They also say that he'll kill you if you show your face at Brí Léith.'

'I don't believe that.'

'Whatever you wish to believe.'

She drew her hands through her loose hair. 'When they came to Brí Léith, I decided to be generous. I would give Midhir the woman freely, openly, with no complaint. I would soon despise him for it.

'But when he kissed me,' she said, her voice breaking, 'when I looked at his face, I saw that he had not become a stupid, coarse beast. He wished me well. They had the same eyes, they were matched, like two horses to a chariot, and I was sick. I had to destroy her.' She grew quiet. 'Bressal, tell me why he has taken no other woman?'

'Why do you ask? Let him be lonely; they're not your arms he wants. He wants nothing from you, only to be left alone.' He set the clay goblet on the floor and stood up from his chair. 'It's late and I'm tired. I'm going to bed. You should sleep too. Forget him and go to sleep.' He patted her shoulder, pulled his cloak about him, and went outside to his sleeping house at the foot of Dowth.

Fuamnach stared at the fire.

'If he still loves me, then the fire will not burn,' she said. She thought of the time that Midhir had made love to her in the reeds beside the river. And Bressal's words to her, 'He can have any woman he wants. All our work will come to nothing. Don't waste yourself for him. Midhir the Proud, Midhir the Beautiful.' That night she had left Dowth, and gone with Midhir to Brí Léith as his wife. 'Why should he not want me still?' She took a blue lizard from a box in the corner of the room, then she threw a handful of salt into the coals. The flames shot up. 'Show me his love! Come to me.' She dropped the lizard in the burning logs and it ran out the back of the hearth.

She went to Bressal's house, stood over his bed and he woke.

'Beautiful anyone until Étaín,' she said. The torch shook in her hand, but she could do nothing to stop it. 'He can't forget her. Bressal, she wasn't beautiful. Her eyes had fever in them. Her skin too white, like the dead.' She laughed, 'Why would he want a strange looking child?'

Bressal took the torch from her and set it into a holder on the wall. 'I saw her sleeping in the reeds beside the river,' he said. 'She was no child. To look at her and not to have her caused me pain; like the sun on the waves of the sea at dawn. Think, Fuamnach, what you have destroyed, and be satisfied.'

'He cannot forget her! You can't have the sun and the sea for your own possessions. How can I make him love me, Bressal? Tell me.'

'Fuamnach, you are the last woman on earth he will love. You've done that yourself.'

'Teach me some spell to make him love me.'

'Your hunger is too great. You had the art, but you wanted him too much.'

She was quiet. She thought of Midhir's voice, of his eyes. 'But he has no woman with him.'

'He's mad, Fuamnach. Everyone says it. Come to my bed; you're shivering. It's cold tonight.' He took her arm and pulled her down to the sheepskins. The hair on his chest was white. 'You look beautiful in that dress; there is no more beautiful woman than you.'

'You're good to me, Bressal.' She kissed him slowly, then drew back, her hands on his shoulders. 'You've always been good to me, kinder than Midhir. But how can we be lovers if I'm so much trouble to you? When I was a queen; then I could have loved you. But now...I have nothing.' She stroked his chest. 'You could bind the Daghdha to come with me to Brí Léith, to stand as surety. He must do it if you ask; because he is your lord and Midhir's, and Midhir has rejected me, and you are my foster-father. Midhir must obey him.' She kissed his shoulders, and then his mouth. 'When I am queen of Brí Léith, then I shall have gifts to bestow,' she said, drawing away from him.

'Goodnight, my friend. Sleep well,' she said softly.

'Your kisses are like the moonlight lying on me; you make it hard to sleep.'

'Soon I'll give you rest. Give me an escort to Brí Léith.'

'I will lose this bargain if you don't come back, Fuamnach.'

'I only want what is my right. Then I'll decide where my kisses go, and who best deserves them.' She smiled at Bressal. 'Shall I damp the fire?'

'No. I'll put it out later. Take that cloak, it's cold.'

She took a heavy fleece cape from a hook on the wall.

'Wake me early, Bressal, so we have a good start for Uisnech. I'll sleep under your sheepskin cloak tonight.'

'My skin is warmer, Fuamnach.'

'I would be safer sleeping in the fire itself, than here with you. Your touch is scorching.'

Bressal laughed.

'You must let me teach you how to damp a fire, some-day,' said Fuamnach, over her shoulder as she went out.

Bressal stared after her, and chuckled. 'Yes; I heard how you cooled Étaín, but I've no wish to drown.'

CHAPTER 3

Truce at Brí Léith

FUAMNACH AND BRESSAL CAMPED below the mountain while the Daghdha and his warriors prepared to lay siege to Brí Léith. But they met no resistance. Fuamnach recognized Midhir's captains in the corn fields, their battlehorses harnessed to plows. The weapon forges were cold; the fortress gate stood open and undefended. So Fuamnach in her torc of twisted gold, like a garrotte cord that quickly breaks the neck, entered the fort with the Daghdha and the warriors of Uisnech.

At the far edge of the courtyard before the mound, she saw a man seated on a wooden bench. He wore a purple fire mask, hiding all the face except for dark eyes, ringed with orange fire. Then the man moved, and Fuamnach saw Midhir's face, and that the mask was a butterfly on his shoulder, its wings outspread and beating the air. Midhir met her eyes and held them, rising, moving toward her.

The Daghdha stepped between them. 'Take care,' he said.

'If it were not for those beside you,' Midhir said to Fuamnach, 'you would not leave Brí Léith alive.'

'I have no wish to leave,' said Fuamnach, her voice shrill.

'Your house is gone,' he said, turning away. 'Destroyed.'

'I'll live in your house here, with you.'

'Fuamnach is your wife,' said the Daghdha, 'and you are under bond not to harm her.'

'She is a murderer.'

'If you have proof of this; if she has destroyed your property, she will pay for it. She has the means. But you have threatened her and now we will not leave Brí Léith until you promise her safety. We mean you no harm; but you must swear this. She has my protection.'

'You are my sworn lord of Uisnech, and my father, and I won't defy you. She can live in my house; but I'd rather see her dead.'

'The slave means so much to you, even now. Étaín is nothing but rot under the leaves,' said Fuamnach. 'Listen to me now; for I speak the truth. I'd be a fool to suffer for a stranger, a girl whom I owe nothing. I would rather do good to myself than to another; so would every man, woman or beast, to survive. Would a starving fox turn from his kill to let another feed instead? Ask any man here; would he lay down his spear as he goes into the battle? He may as well turn his blade on himself. No man becomes king without choosing himself over another. Don't think, because I am a woman, that I must ask nothing for myself. I am mistress of Brí Léith, and your wife, and I won't give that up for some slave that the boy gave you to warm your bed in the Brugh.'

'Your hatred brings us to our senses, Fuamnach,' said Midhir.

'Are you satisfied of your safety, then?' asked the Daghdha.

'I am,' she answered.

'Then I'll leave at daybreak,' and he walked beside her into the hall.

That night the men of Uisnech filled the hall of Brí Léith, and no one went hungry. There was roast meat in the pit fires in the centre of the hall. On the plank tables were broiled onions and leeks piled on copper trays, and white cheese on slabs of quartz. Fresh butter, wrapped in linen and leaves, and wooden casks of ale were brought out of the cold stream below the fort. The night was mild and the fire made the hall warm, so the doors stood open.

When the company took their places at the tables, Fuamnach saw that a place had not been laid for her at Midhir's side. The butterfly perched with folded wings among the carved leaves and flowers of his oak bench. Fuamnach went out of the hall, and when she came back she had a sea-eagle with a red-brown mane tethered to her wrist. She sat down beside Bressal and fed the bird rare beef from her plate.

She saw that Midhir took no food, but spilled his mead into a small gold plate, and the butterfly drank, perched on the rim of the dish. With the bronze meatfork that she had given him at their marriage, a row of kingfishers along the wand, he brought up small morsels of lamb from a cauldron of stew and laid them on the table. The butterfly ate the warm meat, then flew up to the roofbeam. Her wings moved like a flame-coloured bellows above the fire. The Daghdha played his harp quietly. The eagle shuffled her wings and closed her eyes. Then there began a low trilling sound, like the purring of some giant beast, but more liquid. The Daghdha put his harp down, saying, 'None can harm us on the peak of Bri Leith; the nest is safe. Even the pain of my old wounds has ebbed away. What is this creature that lulls us to sleep?'

'It's Étaín,' said Midhir. 'She is alive.'

'He's insane,' said Fuamnach to Bressal.

'Hush! She sings!' said the Daghdha. 'Her wings are fire, all the colors of the flame: gold and copper and silver when it runs liquid in the earth. Her eyes are jewels: sapphire, lapis, topaz, all burning. Her beauty is above all women, and her gentleness beyond all women. We are her young; frail and foolish. Listen to her song, for we shall never be so safe again as in the wake of her wings.'

'I've seen the butterfly in the forest,' said Fuamnach, 'eating the rotten carcass of a hare, searching the mouldering oak leaves for a dead mouse. How lovely she is then.

'Yes, and she longs for your death; for when you are dead she'll make a feast of your flesh, so that she may become strong and give birth to more like her. The flame you love is the funeral pyre, and she draws you to the fire, lulled to danger for her sake, so that you will go eagerly with your fireforged wands to draw blood, to bleed and die. She would lull you with bravery, so that you believe that death is nothing.'

But they didn't hear her. Throughout the hall the men were still, wrapped in the music. Fuamnach drained her cup of wine, and took the eagle under her arm. She touched Bressal's shoulder. 'Come outside with me,' she said.

Bressal followed her. The eagle perched on the top of the wall. Fuamnach leaned against it; she could see the pitfire through the open door of the hall. 'What can I give Midhir? Death, its rancid sweet smell?'

Bressal put his arm around her, and she moved away.

'You have no right. You've taught me nothing.'

Bressal laid his hand on the wall beside her. 'You are beautiful, Fuamnach,' he said slowly, his words slurred with drink. 'Men are weak and want only what the present holds. If Étaín were gone, Midhir would turn to you. But this sickness of his is dangerous. He's not himself; he doesn't eat or sleep.'

Fuamnach stroked the eagle. 'He is ill and his good judgement is gone. I'm his wife; I must judge for him. But she is never out of his sight.'

'Your pet can see in the dark. Wait until the others have gone, tomorrow night.'

'I'll put sleep on his guards.'

'You won't be blamed.'

'And Midhir will be saved. Goodnight, Bressal,' she said, kissing him. 'I'll come to you at Dowth when she is gone.'

CHAPTER 4

Midhir's Chamber

'OUR ORDERS ARE THAT NO ONE is to disturb him,' said the guard before Midhir's chamber, his long handled double axe resting between his feet.

'The Daghdha is leaving now; Midhir will want to say goodbye,' said Fuamnach. She pushed the door open past him, and went into the room.

Midhir lay upon a plain yew wood bench. The room was cold; there was no fire. He had one arm above his head. The butterfly stood on his wrist, its wings lay over his hair and his forehead. It was drinking from his eye. As Fuamnach came into the room it flew up to the window ledge. Midhir stared at nothing.

'He's dreaming,' said the Daghdha. 'Don't speak to him or touch him now. Tell him he has our good will.'

Fuamnach nodded, and they went out, closing the door behind them.

That night the moon was full and huge from the parapet of Brí Léith. Inside the house, the two brothers who stood guard before Midhir's chamber were startled by a sudden shriek. When they got outside they found Fuamnach kneeling on the steps, skinning a hare. Her eagle paced back and forth. Fuamnach said, 'She caught him in the rocks. My knife is dull; I can't do it neatly. Look how the blood stained my cape.'

The guards butchered the hare, and fed the bird bits of meat. It paced and cried for each morsel, neck stretched and beak open. 'Watch her claws,' said Fuamnach, standing over them. When the meat was gone the bird cried. 'Be patient. Now I have some special wine for your work,' she said, smiling at the guards. She unstrung the flask from her neck and gave it to them. 'It's the Daghdha's own wine. Have you never tasted it?' One of the guards tilted back the flask and sent a fine arc of pale liquid into his mouth. 'It tastes like flowers,' he said. 'Like honey,' said the other. They sat down on the steps.

'Have you ever seen the moon so close and red?' whispered Fuamnach, standing behind them, her hands on their shoulders. 'Like a shield on a wall.'

'Blood on the moon means rain,' said one of the guards. He shook the flask and squeezed it. It was empty. 'We should go back. Maybe the king is dying.' 'He looks dead already,' said the other.

'Wait,' said Fuamnach, taking the flask. 'I'll get some more. Stay here, so I can find you.'

Inside the hall was dark, with only one lamp at the end of the passage, behind the door of Midhir's chamber. Before the door she heard a noise and stopped. There was a rustling in the thatch above. The eagle cocked her head and stared.

'Only brown bats,' she whispered, 'Not now. I have another treat for you, inside.'

She opened the door carefully. Midhir lay still on his bed of skins, his arms by his sides, his eyes open and staring. There was no butterfly on the window ledge. Fuamnach stepped into the room and closed the door behind her. Then she turned around.

In the corner of the room, opposite Midhir's bed, a dragon coiled and seethed, watching her with orange eyes the size of fists. Silver-green scales glittered over muscle as she moved, rising up to her height at the ceiling. Smoke poured from her jaws and wound across the floor of the room.

Fuamnach took one step toward Midhir. The dragon roared like a bonfire as it takes straw and kindling. The floor of the room was a lake of fire. The eagle screamed, tore at its tether, clawing Fuamnach's arm. The bird flew to the ceiling, and out the window.

'Nathrach, serpent of water,
You guard him, but try to keep him.
I will hold him with my body.
Étaín, I will wake him.'

She went out of the room, slammed the door and ran down the hall, calling the guards. They came quickly to Midhir's room. The room was dim with fog. Midhir hadn't moved, and the butterfly stood on his chest, its wings glistening with fog. Fuamnach walked past them out of the house.

She took Étaín's mare from the stable. Outside the fortress gate she rode left, around the wall. When she reached the gate again she struck the mare hard with her rowan stick. The mare reared up and came down with a shock. Fuamnach backed the mare a few paces, then halted, and got down. The mare stood trembling. Water filled the sickle marks of her front hooves, then ran over.

Before long the moon was visible in the pool, like a clean, new-tanned bodhran. Fuamnach knelt at the edge of the water. She put the stick into the middle of the moon's reflection, until her wrist disappeared, and she couldn't touch bottom. The air was still on the mountain; not a breath of wind moved the surface of the water. She sat back on her heels and stirred the water with her stick. Now clouds drifted slowly across the moon's face. She sang,

> 'Turn, spindle of sky,
> Spindle of dark sky.
> Wind the clouds,
> Turn the stars,
> Make me a storm.
>
> Spindle of wind,
> Turn on the mountain top,
> Make a storm.
>
> Fly, water, over the trees.
> Sweep the sky,
> Drown the stones,
> Make a storm.'

The pool went dark. The mare was a dim shape close by; wind ruffled her mane, the grass. Fuamnach sang softly,

> 'Who will come swim with me?
> Deep down the current is cold;
> But there are jewels there

For one who is bold.
While the others sleep,
Come ride; the waves are rising.
Take my mane and go deep.'

Then something began to come up out of the pool. Its head came first, shaped like a horse, with black water streaming off of it, and pale round eyes, like a fish. Its mane was long and dank and as it rose higher, drenched, it seemed to shed its skin of black water, and its body was pale, smooth, and it coiled as the water churned.

Fuamnach screamed and ran into the fort. Then the storm struck. It was hard to see, or move. Leaves ripped from branches and thatch torn loose from buildings flew against her face and arms. She crouched beneath the wall, and watched the roof of Midhir's house fly off, piece by piece. People and animals ran for shelter. The rain came down in waves sideways. Soon she could see nothing at all. The sound of wind and rain on the mountain was like the sound of the sea breaking against cliffs, and it seemed to Fuamnach that if the rain didn't stop, they would drown.

The next day Midhir and Fuamnach pulled bodies out of the water and from collapsed houses, and led animals to high ground. Still the wind blew hard and Samhain passed with no mast for pigs nor grain for horses or for bread. When the days grew long again the wind and cold kept on and the grass didn't grow. Cows starved in the pasture and were driven into the woods and up into the mountains, but their ribs showed at midsummer, and then the people bled them to feed their children. There were no fairs held, with little to trade and the roads over the bogs overgrown with thistles, or washed out by flood. Cows were butchered for meat, and many men drowned fishing the rough seas. Midhir led his men in raids to the west and south; his horses grew thin and he drove them hard, looking for food. Fuamnach waited with the other women, hoping for a bony calf or a ram, but there was none to be found. One by one Midhir's horses were slaughtered to feed his people. There were children who had known nothing but wind and rain and thunder, for whom summer and a day of sun, or a field of long grass were only stories.

CHAPTER 5

The Brugh of Aonghus

FOR SEVEN YEARS the storm kept on and there was not a tree or a mountain or any high place where the butterfly could light and rest; only the bare rocks of the sea. But at the end of the seventh year, Aonghus found the butterfly, her wings ragged and torn, on the sill over the entrance of the Brugh.

He took her gently from the ledge and put her on his cloak, saying,

'Fair Étaín,
How far have you wandered
From your rich bed, from Midhir,
Whose need of you
Burned forests,
Drove rivers to the sea?

Midhir dreams; Étaín lost; his corn fails.
The bones of his horses ash,
Mixed with earth in the fallow fields.
Below, in the river,
My horses turn with the tide,

Their manes like sea grass,
Their cold eyes stones.
In the north your father's stables are empty.

How far have I failed in my swearing
Since I took you from your father's house?
Étaín, you shall be fair again,
And from this day mistress of the Brugh.
The Boyne will run red with blood
Before any harm you again.'

He took her into the passage, and brought her herbs and water. That night the wind and the rain stopped, and within a month there were wildflowers in the woods and the meadows. He gathered violets and yellow kingcups and honey and brought them into the Brugh, while she couldn't fly. When she grew stronger and her colour brighter Aonghus put her into a cage made of crystal. He carved her image into the ledge above the threshold: linked wings; and he slept beside her every night. No one was permitted to enter the Brugh but Aonghus.

But when Bressal came to the Brugh to kindle the new fire on Samhain eve, he saw the threshold carved with butterflies, and he sent word to Fuamnach that Étaín was found, and alive.

Fuamnach was sleeping in Midhir's chamber when Bressal's messenger arrived. She and Midhir had been awake all night with the rites of Samhain, and it was past noon when Fuamnach left his bed and saw the messenger waiting for her in the great hall. She led him outside to the parapet; the air was soft and sweet on Brí Léith. Below were men driving oxen pulling loads of cut grain; they waved greetings to her.

'How is the lord Bressal?' asked Fuamnach.

'Well,' the boy answered, giving Fuamnach parchment, tied with a strand of black yarn. She unrolled it. It was a drawing of the Brugh with a butterfly above the entrance to the passage, in dark ink of alder. 'Who else have you shown this to, today?'

'No one, I swear.'

She unclasped a brooch from the front of her cape, and put the sharp pin against the back of his neck.

'Think carefully. Make no mistake. Speak a lie and I'll know by the change of colour in your eyes. Close your eyes and I'll know by your breath. Hold your breath and I'll know by the heat in your skin. Don't lie, boy, or your life is ended. Does anyone in Brí Léith know of this?'

'No one, lady.'

'Good,' she said, releasing him. 'Go to Dowth while I watch you ride. Don't stop until you get there.' She put the brooch in his hand. 'Thank your lord Bressal, and tell him I'm coming. Now go!'

When Fuamnach could no longer see him she went to her own chamber. She plaited her hair in seven braids, then coiled them and tied them with strands of copper. She put on a tunic of dark green silk, and a heavy vest of linked copper mail over it. She fastened a belt of copper and green marble around her waist, and tucked a knife with a narrow blade into it. Then she went into Midhir's room.

He slept naked as he fought, the scars on his chest and thighs blurred by morning light. Fuamnach touched his shoulder and he woke.

'Fuamnach, why are you dressed?' he asked. 'Come back to bed.'

'I dreamt last night of Étaín.'

Midhir turned over. She ran her hand through his hair. 'In my dream she lives.'

'Often in dreams the dead are living,' he said. 'It's Samhain. Don't trust what you see.'

'I see only my shame, Midhir.'

'Why do you speak of it?'

'I have no peace.'

'I brought her here myself,' he said, his voice low. 'Only Étaín was innocent.'

Fuamnach got up from the bed. 'I'll bring her to you, Midhir. I know she's alive.'

Midhir stared at her.

'I'm going now, to get her. You must do something as well, Midhir,' she said. 'Make peace with Aonghus. You loved him. As your own son. Ask him to come now, to make peace with you. He can't refuse you, Midhir. Mend what you can, before it's too late.'

Midhir took her wrist. 'I've never dreamt of her.'

'When we die we'll sleep soundly,' said Fuamnach, leaning over him, taking his kiss on her cheek, knowing that his lips would meet hers with an exact, measured pressure. She stepped back from him, her eyes wet. 'Will you send for him?'

'Take guards with you, Fuamnach.'

She shook her head. 'Send for him now, before I go.' Then while Fuamnach stayed in his room, he sent a messenger to the Brugh to bring Aonghus to him, and then Fuamnach left his house.

She rode fast over the bogs, galloping along the river beside the banks of ferns gone copper with frost, and grey-leaved willows, until she stood on the top of the mound of Dowth.

She turned her horse toward the west, facing the Brugh. The valley was filled with mist between them.

'Now shall our torment be ended, Étaín, loved by Midhir, loved by Aonghus. Midhir lies; he dreams of you every night; he drinks poison foxglove to sleep again. I have heard him call your name a hundred times. Nights I have lain awake, fearing you lived, and would return to take him. Now, for one moment, before Midhir knows, you are mine.'

She turned and saw Bressal walking up the mound, his cloak swinging out wide in the wind.

'Welcome, Fuamnach,' he said. 'We're honoured by your visit. I must let Aonghus know that you're here.' His hair was completely white, but he stood straight in the wind, still broad in the chest, the muscles clear in his arms.

She got down, and put her arms inside his cloak. 'I'd rather go inside with you, Bressal, where it's warm.'

'How strange that he, too, has company from Brí Léith; a messenger, I think. I saw Midhir's grey horse before dusk.'

'Have they left again?'

'Why do you ask? What are you planning?'

'To drink wine with you tonight,' she said, rubbing her head against his chest.

He took her chin in his hand. 'If you go near Étaín, Aonghus will kill you.'

'I've no desire to see Aonghus.'

'Still, I should let him know you are here.'

'Not tonight, Bressal. Haven't you missed me?' She drew her hands down the length of his back.

Bressal took her horse's reins, and they walked down the mound to his house. They tied the horse to a thorn tree, and went into his chamber.

Fuamnach left Bressal's bed when it was dark. She dressed quietly. When she found her knife and put it in her belt, Bressal stirred, and lit a lamp.

'Where are you going, Fuamnach?'

'Why did you send the messenger, Bressal?'

He got up and put his cloak around him. 'Not to see your death.'

'If you go to Aonghus, he will certainly kill me.'

'Aonghus is gone. What does it matter now? Come back to bed.'

'Aonghus has gone to Brí Léith. I pity him; he could have saved her if he had not hidden her away. He's afraid of losing her to Midhir.'

'Fuamnach, what will you gain? I'm old; don't let me see your death,' he said, holding her arms.

'Let go of me!' She pulled free and started to the door.

'Don't! Listen to me, Fuamnach.' He caught her again. 'Do you know why Dowth is called the Mound of Darkness?'

'Let go!'

'You will listen,' he said, shaking her, and speaking quickly. 'I made a pact with the men of this land for gold if they would work one day to build my house. And my own sister set a spell on the sun so it wouldn't set, and the men worked long to finish my house. But while they worked I took my sister to bed, and then the spell broke and night came, and she called this place Darkness. But you must know that she had a child, and that day she died, and you must know that you are my own daughter, Fuamnach, and I won't lose you.'

She stared at him for a long moment, then struck him in the face. He let go of her. She picked up a heavy carved rock, seeing the fragile bones of his face, the crack of bone, the shudder of impact in her arm very near. 'Everything I know you taught me. What I will do now I learned from you.' She turned away from him, facing the door. 'Who are those people who sit by their fires tonight? I would give gold to be one of them, to work, to drive my cattle, to bear children. To be free of your words.' She faced him again. He hadn't moved. 'But I am free of you, Bressal, of your touch, because of Midhir. I hear his voice. I see his eyes. I feel his skin only. Midhir is beautiful, so I would not give gold.' She left the house.

The mist was coming in over the river, lying thick against the hills. She rode close to the river, through the shorn brown reeds, passing cows huddled in the grass. She stopped her horse under a willow tree beside the water.

'Midhir, stay by the far shore, where I can't see your face. Stand and wait for your destruction, this tide of suffering that will come soon, lapping at your feet: Étaín, drowned.'

She dismounted, broke a branch from the tree and stirred the water.

'Now rise, wind,
Tear limbs, leaves, wings.
Let me hear the roar
Of death's dark wing
Across the night sky.
Make a storm
To set the captive free.'

The Brugh was easy to find; there were torches beside the opening of the mound. She carried the crystal shelter outside, and hit it with the stone from Dowth, but the stone cracked and fell apart. She picked up the cage and smashed it against the entrance stone, and the butterfly flew away.

From behind the mound of the Brugh, a dark cloud rose up, like a beast lifting its head from sleep. On the river Boyne the waves blew back toward the sea, and the brown reeds and the willows bent down beneath the wind. Fuamnach turned back to Dowth.

CHAPTER 6

The Storm

AT INBER CICHMAINE, at the house of the chieftain Étar at the edge of the sea, the wind struck hard. Étar's people, who had been eating and drinking in their hall, were quiet, listening to the roar of the storm against the roof. Suddenly the doors blew open and the torches went out. When they were relit from the cooking fire, leaves and debris covered the floor of the hall. The doors were bolted shut, and Étar sent his slaves to fill the wine cups all around, although the company was already drunk. From a bronze vat his servants poured wine. They didn't notice a drowned butterfly that had blown in with the storm and fallen into the wine vat, and when they served Étar's wife, the butterfly was poured into her goblet. Although she saw it in the wine, she said nothing because she was drunk, and she didn't want to be laughed at by her husband's people. When she drank, it slipped down her throat.

Midhir watched all day for Aonghus, and when he saw his foster-son appear on the road, he met him at the gate with his shield and spear raised. Aonghus saluted with his own weapons, and Midhir embraced him.

Then he said, 'Come inside out of the wind,' and Aonghus replied, 'I'll be glad to see Fuamnach.'

'She's not here, but it was her wish that you and I be reconciled. On Samhain she dreamt of Étaín, and she's gone in search of her. But if Étaín were alive, Fuamnach would destroy her, no matter what she says to me.'

Aonghus grasped Midhir's arm. 'Don't let your anger rise against me, Midhir. Étaín is alive. She has been with me since the long winter ended. In the Brugh I hid her, in that shape she had when the storm blew her from your house. Don't hold me now; let me go quickly.'

'If Étaín is lost, don't spare Fuamnach. I'm bound not to raise my hand against her; nor can my anger be against you, but some trick of earth that I must lose what I love, again and again. Ride fast, Aonghus.'

He helped him up on his grey stallion, and when Aonghus had taken up the reins, and turned him towards the east, Midhir struck the horse with his whip, and the horse leapt away.

'Fly to the Hall of Aonghus;
Be quick.
Let Étaín see the shadow,
Hear the breath taken and held.
Move from the target,
From the moment of striking.
Watch, beware.'

From the mound Midhir watched the storm. Dark clouds rolled in the east. But by dusk he saw that the storm was passing away.

'Oh, she's dead, Aonghus. I know it. Drowned. Why do you ride fast? I'll sleep and dream no more. Now beautiful Étaín rests, safe for a time.'

He struck the ground with his yew staff. The forest below the rath was illuminated. 'But now, Fuamnach, you shall be afraid.'

As he spoke, fog reached the mountain and wrapped it around, hiding Brí Léith from all eyes. Midhir went into his house and waited.

Aonghus rode hard all night, and as dawn approached, he reached the valley of the Boyne. The standing stones around the Brugh were silvered with rain. Beside the entrance stone he found the cage, smashed and empty. He found the deep hoofprints of Fuamnach's horse, where the rain had not blurred them, and followed them east along the river. Then he sent Midhir's horse running to Dowth.

He saw Bressal with a company of druids before the entrance of the mound of Dowth that looked west towards the Brugh. Fuamnach was sweeping leaves away from the curbstones that ringed the mound. Aonghus rode straight up the hill, his spear held high in his right hand. Bressal saw him coming, and moved toward Fuamnach, but she pushed him away. She threw herself forward, her arms stretched out with her weight against a curbstone, and Aonghus let the spear fly. It went straight through her back and cracked the stone.

Aonghus rode up to the stone, and turned the horse sideways, so that he sat high above Fuamnach. Bressal screamed. Aonghus caught up a mass of her red hair with one hand and pulled her head back, baring the neck. He swung his sword down and sliced skin, muscle and with another sweep cut through the bone, and took her head.

The horse's chest was sprayed with bright blood. He reached down over the horse's withers and tied the head onto the leathers by the hair.

He wrenched his spear free from Fuamnach's back. Then Bressal grabbed his belt, to pull him down. Aonghus turned the horse, and sent his spear through Bressal's chest, dropping him. He pulled the cloak off Bressal and covered Fuamnach's body. Then he rode down the hill.

He rode slowly along the Boyne until he came to a wide bank. He cleaned his sword and his spear in the grass, and walked his horse into the river, to wash the blood clean. He let the blood drain away from Fuamnach's head in the current, until the river was clear, and the vessels of the neck were clean. And all the things that lived along the Boyne and in the sea tasted Fuamnach's blood: the salmon in the river, and the men who ate the salmon, deer and bear drinking at dawn and dusk, women bathing in the river and washing their husbands' clothes, and the dragonflies and copper moths that drank from the quiet pools. All these tasted her bitterness and her triumph, and her love for Midhir. And the salt of her blood mixed with the salt of everything that lived and died in the river and the sea.

When Aonghus got to the Brugh, he made a small cage out of the broken limbs of the shelter for Fuamnach's head, so it would dry and to keep it safe from the crows. He hung his foster-mother's head beside the door of his house so that all who came to the Brugh na Bóinne would know that Aonghus had kept his word and avenged Étaín's death.

BOOK III – THE HILLFORTS

CHAPTER 1

The Estuary

IN THE RECKONING OF MEN one thousand years had passed since Bóinn and the Daghda had met in the Brugh, and Étaín Horse-Rider set her stallion loose among the mares in Meath. The carved stones of the Brugh were hidden by earth and grass. The ash tree was felled by wind on the hill of Uisnech, and the rampart on Brí Léith collapsed, burying the entrance to the mound. Still there were men and women who claimed to see a king walking on top of a hill at dusk or dawn, and it was believed by many of the peoples, the horse riders, the deer people, and the boar people, that the old ones were still alive, but kept themselves hidden in the mounds, in the Sidhe.

The Laigin, a people much skilled at war with iron weapons, built forts on the mounds of Dowth and Knowth, and warriors rose among them to subjugate the old tribes, and draw tribute from all the chieftains. And some of these claimed themselves High King from the ancient meeting place at Tara.

In that time a child was born to the wife of Étar of the old tribes. She was a girl with yellow hair, blue eyes and dark brows. They called her Étaín, and she was raised by Etar in his house by the sea. It was said that she was the most beautiful child who had ever been born in Ireland.

One afternoon in summer, when Étaín was twelve years old, she was bathing in the estuary called Inber Cichmaine. The sky was broad and blue and cloudless. The children of Etar's house were catching frogs in cups and making boats of hazelnut shells with swan's down for sails. Étaín was swimming along the shore.

When she stood up, the saltwater streaming from her hair, the reeds around her thighs, she saw a strange horse-man on the bank above. All the children had stopped to watch him.

He sat upon a broad shouldered brown horse with huge hooves and a curling mane and tail, who pranced and sidestepped, and shook his head against the bit, eager to run. The rider tapped the horse with his heels and tightened the reins and the horse stood still.

The man wore a green cloak over a scarlet tunic embroidered with gold, with a gold brooch on each shoulder of the cloak, and a span of creased gold connecting them. In his hand he held a five-pronged bronze spear with bands of gold around it from the haft to the socket. His hair was bright gold, his brows black, and his eyes the colour of deep sea, with sadness in them. He did not greet them, but talked to himself or the air, and he looked at Étaín and named her.

He said,

'This is Étaín here today,
She who lives in the mountain of pale women
Where the moon and the swans sleep.
Here among little children is she,

On the brink of Inber Cichmaine.

It is she who healed the King's eye
From the well of Loch Da Lig
In the Brugh of Aonghus.
It is she who was swallowed in the drink
In the beaker of the wife of Etar.

Because of her the King shall chase
The swans from Tara.
Because of her the King
Shall drown his two horses
In the pool of Loch Da Airbrech.

For her, forests were burned and cleared,
Lakes drained and rivers forged to the sea.
For her shall fields be planted
And chariots go by roads
In woods where only foxes travel.

For her there shall be war
Against Eochaidh of Meath;
The Sidhe mounds will be destroyed
And many thousands will do battle.

It is she that was sung of in the land.
It is she the king is seeking.
Once she was called Bé Find,
Now she is our Étaín.'

He looked one long moment more at Étaín, and the air
grew cold. Then he raised his spear, turned his horse and

galloped away. Étaín watched him until he was a speck on the distant plain. She said nothing to her parents about the horseman, because it was her father's wish that she be kept inside, out of the view of men, and she loved to walk alone along the estuary, watching the herons and the swans.

Seven summers passed, and Eochaidh King of Tara came with his thousand warriors to Inber Cichmaine, and they struck hard. It was no raid for cattle or horses. Cattle stood in the grass while the wounded thrashed and moaned on the banks of Inber Cichmaine, and Eochaidh did not hold his warriors back from killing.

For the promise of Étaín, Eochaidh spared Étar. He wanted the girl for his wife, for he had taken hostages to Tara, there guarded by his brother Ailill in the old fort that Eochaidh had restored, and he had declared himself High King of Ireland. But no chieftain would send him tribute until Eochaidh held the feis of Tara, the sacred marriage. And for that he would wed Étaín, for it was said that no woman was as beautiful as Étaín, though few had seen her.

The morning after the battle when Étar submitted to Eochaidh, the banks of Inber Cichmaine were still. Light came on the hill beyond the estuary, green and gold where the sun touched it, moving over the hill, searching in dark crevasses, and in the water too, quietly, without disturbing the surface; looking carefully for something below, something or someone lost. Then a crane took off from the banks, rippling the mirror, and the first sound of keening for the dead rose up and the day was broken.

Eochaidh walked among the dead, leading his heavy roan horse along the bank, his warriors greeting him as they struck trophies from Étar's fallen, leaving the headless

trunks for the fire. He passed Étar and his captain lifting
the body of a kinsman onto a cart. Two slaves who had not
run away pulled the cart away, downwind, to the bonfire.

When the wounded horses had been killed, and the hill
and the water were drenched with sunlight, Eochaidh
found white-haired Étar beside the fire and they went into
the hall. The walls were bare where shining weapons had
hung; Eochaidh's guards who stood beside the door now
carried swords with Étar's mark on them.

Eochaidh and Étar sat with their wounds throbbing at
the long table. Both men still wore their armour; in the
silences the leather and bronze and gilded silver made
small sounds of war. Eochaidh spoke slowly.

'You shouldn't mourn, Étar. You're an old man now,
with many heads over your threshold; your time of battle
is over. Rest now. It's no shame to fall against my men; no
one in this land has stood against me.

'Now see how the dead of your family are honoured.
Their blood will serve the land; for your daughter will sit
beside me and be my wife, and we have put an end to war.
Your goblets will be lined with gold, and you shall have
horses out of my own stallions. For I've heard in every place
that there's no gold more beautiful than Étaín's hair. But
now Étar's daughter must be hidden no more.' He reached
across the table for Étar's arm, to touch it, and the motion
brought a jolt of pain; but Étar moved his hand away, and
took hold of his empty cup.

'Grief makes women ugly,' said Étar. 'That's what
you've brought her. And when will you take her?'

'I've sent horsemen to every corner of Ireland with the
news; I'll hold the feis of Tara at Samhain.'

'So soon?' He closed his eyes and sighed. 'With luck
maybe you won't be alive by Samhain. I think you'll be

murdered by the first man who comes near you with a weapon.' For a moment he was silent. His skin was damp and pale, his breath coming hard. 'I've agreed that Étaín is yours; I have no power to hold her now. But you won't keep her. Perhaps there are some who think that Tara has found a king, but I see only a butcher with a gift for lies. You dream and take the sleeping lies for truth. The fort of Tara will lie in ruins again.'

Eochaidh stood and smoothed back his copper hair. He spoke lightly and quickly. 'I've heard bitter words before from old men who crouched before my sword. I pity you. Your strength is gone from you. I will survive the feis of Tara, I will make Étaín the treasure of Ireland, while you lie cold in the earth. I won't waste my words on you. Go to bed, and send your daughter to me with wine.'

'Send your guards instead; the wine is yours now.'

'I want to see the girl.'

Étar didn't answer.

'What are you hiding from me? Has she damaged herself? If she is dead by her own hand, or by yours, you won't survive her.'

'I can't keep grief from her,' he said, dully. A woman came into the hall and knelt before the hearth, working a carved hide bellows. 'Send Étaín to me,' Étar said, and she left the room. Eochaidh watched the turf smoulder. He heard someone enter the room, and turned to look.

Étaín's yellow hair, pulled out from its long braids, was loose and matted with straw, her black mourning clothes soiled. But in the dark hall her skin shone as if she stood before a bonfire. Her arms were as white as sickle moons, the bones of her face delicate, her cheeks and mouth red. Her brows were black, her eyes, that looked at him with hatred, blue as lapis. Étar had been wise to keep her hidden.

She set a bowl down on the table between them. She dipped the amethyst cups into the wine and raised them to the firelight, to see that they were filled equally. She set Eochaidh's cup next to his hand; he took her wrist. The thought of mounting her, of his skin next to her luminous skin, made him uneasy. For all her beauty her looks were strange; it was hard to believe she was the daughter of the old man who sat across from him. He pulled her down beside him on the bench. She didn't resist him, but sat very still, looking away. Then she turned her head slowly, meeting his gaze, staring at him. He wondered if she were mad; great beauty was unlucky.

'When the foreign kings pay tribute at the harbours of Ireland,' said Eochaidh, standing, with his palms flat on the table, 'they will hear of Étaín; they'll see her and dream of her while they sleep with their queens.' He drew a long breath that seared him. Tears came into his eyes, and he let them fall.

'Étar, you fought too long and hard against me. It was no even match; why wouldn't you give in? You forced me to kill every son and brother and cousin; your stubborness forced me. But now I see that it was fate, the only way. They gave their lives for peace. Had you sent me a hostage yesterday you could have prevented their deaths. But I knew you wouldn't send a hostage, Etar. This battle was for Étaín. She will bring only good things to the land, no deformed children or lambs, no stunted wheat, only perfect, whole things. She'll bring an end to war in Ireland, and for that reason I had to slaughter your family.'

Étar said nothing.

Eochaidh sat down. He drank, looking at Étaín's skin, the shape of her neck. He was sure that only a few aged warriors, now passing their days among dreams and kettles of sweet porridge, had more skulls of name above their doors, where new-hatched ravens poked and played among the eyeholes, than he at thirty and in his prime. He thought how no one had ever defeated him at chariot or mounted combat, and that he had let no woman keep him.

He knew that Étaín hoped only now that he would not kill her parents, not take every cow and pig; not climb the high pastures and find the stallion and the mares, or the ram and the ewes above. She was no different from any other; he had heard them beg in all ways; only he needed no hostages from Étar, so he had been harsh. And her father who had let no strange man see her or talk to her put his head down in his arms upon the table and slept.

CHAPTER 2

Preparations at Tara

EOCHAIDH LEFT HALF of Étar's cattle and pigs to him, but he gave all the horses to Étaín for her bride price. At Tara the goldsmith made a torc of pure red gold for her, with vines and leaves and horses intertwined. When it was finished the druid Fedach took it for safekeeping, so that no covetous eyes should look upon it, and lessen its power of protection.

Tara was transformed, keeping pace with the days, as Samhain approached and birds gathered in chattering hordes in the trees, then, in a single great wave, left the woods empty and silent. The old road that led from the woods and the well to the standing stone Lia Fáil at the foot of the Mound of the Hostages was cleared of grass and brush and cut again. Wooden pillars were erected along the road, so that a roof of red silk could be lashed between them. Eochaidh raised a pavilion on the mound; his hostages, the sons and brothers of the chieftains of the land, had the place of honour to witness the feis of Tara, though they were bound in chains. When the chieftains came to acknowledge Eochaidh as High King, or to watch him fail, they would see that those who had been taken from them as surety were alive.

In the weeks before Samhain, Eochaidh went nowhere without guard. When Fedach, who watched the Mound at dawn, counted nine days before Samhain by the sunbeam on the cave wall, there were tents raised in the shelter of the royal hall, and caravans of horsemen and carts filled the roads to Tara. There were roasting pits dug, grain from Etar for the horses of the chieftains, and wine from Gaul. The people who farmed and grazed the land below the hill said that Tara's greatness had come again.

Étaín's mares appeared on the road from the coast, and Eochaidh had them driven into the fields apart from his own horses. When her chariot arrived it was escorted to a house below the fort, and Étaín herself was hidden, so that no one could look on her and cast a spell upon her. Then Eochaidh went into his tent with his brother Ailill, and took his last meal of meat and wine before the fasting that would end with the cup he took from her hands in the solemn rite.

'The druid from Cruachan is the ugliest man I've ever seen,' said Ailill, turning toward the fire, the long jagged scar from a boar's tusk shining on his thigh. 'Tonight they meet to discuss the High King's prohibitions—your geis. You give them too much power.'

Eochaidh shook his head. 'If they want to keep it they'll be reasonable.'

'I couldn't agree to live by their whim before I knew it.'

'There's no other way to bind the tribes.' He filled Ailill's cup again.

'And when you embrace the people, will your army still follow you?'

Eochaid stared at him. 'My men wake with me as they wake with the sun and sleep when they go to their beds of clay. They grow rich and bleed and rot. We're all warriors, Ailill. There's nothing to be afraid of.'

'When the tribes blame you, not the gods, for their troubles, then I will be afraid.'

'You saw how easily Étar submitted. He couldn't bring himself to risk everything against me, because he suspected that I was the rightful High King. The old man is wise. I see how this thing will be done; it's inevitable.' He looked out the door of the tent, at the flares moving past on the roads below and across the fields. 'Tonight all those fires will be put out. I have been careful; all will be well.'

But that night Eochaidh couldn't sleep. At midnight a low horn, like a beast under the sea, gave the signal to extinguish all fires. He put a plain cloak around him and went outside. From the trees behind his tent he watched the fires go out. The camp fires of the chieftains who had travelled to the feis, the guard fires around the fort and the house where Étaín, a maid, as Fedach had made certain, waited for him; the fire beside his own tent, and below, in the fields where the animals slept and grazed, the small fires to keep wolves away—all these went dark. And although he couldn't see them, he knew that in the hearth of each small house ashes were stirred and smothered, so that not even a spark remained.

Eochaidh went into the field, and lay down in the grass. It seemed to him that this night was no different from any night when he had waited for morning, for a battle; but that no night would be the same after. He would never lie on the rough ground again, waiting for the light, so full of desire for what other men feared. He would not meet death on his terms again. What had he bartered? The heaviness of the wine settled on him, and he slept. He dreamt of a

slamming mountain that parted and closed, with the blood,
feathers and sinew of crushed birds on its granite mouth,
and no rhythm to its opening, so that he must fly through,
with nothing but his luck.

While Eochaidh slept the white mare called from the pasture, and Étaín left her bed. The women sleeping on the
floor around her bed didn't stir when she stepped quietly
around them, taking a halter from a hook on the wall,
wrapping a cloak about her. At the door of the house she
stopped and looked out; her guards stood with their backs
to her. She walked quietly past them through the trees
toward the dark pasture. She walked by the great hall, and
the open pits for boar and deer for the wedding feast. She
stopped under a tree and looked across the field at the tents
of the chieftains.

'Sleep, strangers.
Sleep, father and mother by the sea.
There are too many warriors.
So am I tonight;
One man would not be hard to kill
While he sleeps beside me.
But father, who would sleep and wake after?
Samhain's gate swings open and
Death comes in: not now.
When I walk this way again,
I will not be Étaín.'

The white mare galloped along the wicker fence; she
stopped and neighed, and ran back toward the trees. She
turned again and came to Étaín at the fence. Étaín leaned
back against the mare's chest, and put her arms around her

head, her cheek against the mare's jaw. 'Are you looking for the other horses? Don't worry,' she said, 'they're not far away.' She turned and breathed the mare's own breath, and blew softly across the mare's nostrils. The horse grew very still.

Étaín slipped the halter over the mare's head, took a fist of mane and swung herself up onto the horse. She couldn't see the ground, the field was so dark; there might have been waves as well as earth under her. But the mare was the same colour as the moon, smooth and pure as the palest gold that has been burned through and shed every grain of earth. She laid her hands on the mare's shoulder to feel the warmth and weight of the animal that would not rise up into the sky.

The mare wanted to go forward, tossing her head back and down to shed the reins, and Étaín gave them, pressing her legs gently into the horses's sides, sending her on. At each stroke of the canter she let herself fall and be caught again; then she could feel the mare's head go down and her back round, and move into a floating trot.

When they were tired Étaín stopped her and slipped off. With the reins hooked in her arm, she combed the horse's mane with her fingers.

'Tomorrow is our wedding day,
I'll braid your mane with gold.
A collar of gold for you and me,
And chains for the hostages
While they watch.

When he comes to take you
Don't run, or fight him.
Keep still as a torch

In a place with no wind.'

She ran her hand down the mare's side; her white coat was heavy with winter coming. 'Here the winter grass is thick; your ribs will not show in Tara.'

The mare moved her head listening; there was a sound in the far corner of the field, at the edge of the woods. Étaín said, 'There's nothing there; there's no one.' The mare called again. 'Stay here. Will you go looking for wolves? There's nothing there,' said Étaín, but the mare galloped away. Clouds covered the moon, and the mare disappeared; she didn't return. Étaín went back to her bed.

The house beside the grove was called the Queen's Bed, and it stood on a small hill with a granite stone the length of a man lying below. There were circular depressions cut into the rock, and at Bealtaine, fresh milk was poured into the bowls, and over the ground. No men were allowed in the Queen's Bed, and it was there that every bride of a High King had slept before her marriage. Small white river stones were laid around the house, and striped shells, the kind they called dogwhelk that were crushed with the living creature inside, and the garments of kings were soaked in its clear blood, so that royal purple came into them after three days in the sun. The house was old and the timbers grey and plain; there were no tapestries on the lime-washed walls. There was a funnel in the roof that let the rain come into a small bathing pit lined with stones, some scorched from heat; it drained out of the house again and washed the stones below.

Everything was scrubbed clean. But there were only plank benches to sit on, and mattresses stuffed with heather for sleeping, with rough blankets, like the summer camps above Étaín's home. The women of Eochaidh's tribe slept on the floor in a circle around her bed; their bare arms and copper bracelets and red hair shone above the blankets. Beside Étaín's bed, a plain box of apple wood held the wedding garments: the green silk tunic and purple fleece cloak, the box of powdered blue-green malachite to paint her eyes, and Eochaidh's gifts – the two gold torcs, one for her neck and the other for the mare, a rowan whip, and a bridle with gold fastenings.

Étaín watched the moon through the smoke hole in the ceiling until it passed out of the circle. It seemed she would never sleep. There was a soft scraping sound on the other side of the wall; a stag moved his antlers slowly against the house, rubbing off the velvet. It started to rain lightly on the roof, and she closed her eyes.

A man leaned over her, spreading out his cape to cover her. His cloak was dark, transparent purple, and she could see it glisten, and the veins of his arms running through it, a great sweeping wing. She woke suddenly and sat up. The room was dark, and the rain still falling.

The old woman who had been Eochaidh's nurse came to her bed. 'Can't you sleep?' she whispered. 'It's the same for us all, before the day. I had terrible dreams for a week after, the way I'd wake myself screaming and my husband thought I was mad. It will pass. Will you tell me your dream?'

Étaín stared into the dark, hugging her knees.

'I hate the eve of Samhain with the watchfires put out,' said the woman, 'but there's nothing that could come into this house. No wolf could pass the guards Eochaidh has put below. I saw their spears pointing up in the moonlight a while back when I looked outside; not a mouse could get past them.' Étaín got up and looked out the door. Three guards stood under the yews in the streaming rain. 'But it's cruel with no fire, and when you're cold it's hard to sleep,' said the nurse. She held the soft white blanket up, and Étaín lay down, and the woman covered her.

'There, will you sleep with music?' she asked, smoothing Étaín's hair. She picked up a wooden flute and played a low song, a slow searching air that went out into the woods, winding about the roots of trees and over the moss, and into the branches and leaves, slowly, like a solemn dance, hand over hand, and from the trees into the cleared fields where the horses walked in the wind, and beyond, out over the waves, where all the dreams move shoulder to shoulder, and the moon shines on them.

The rain fell lightly, waking Eochaidh. He touched his weapons first, as he always did on waking, coming awake fully in an instant, listening for a sound which might have warned him in sleep of man or beast approaching. But there was nothing, just rain and the dark hillside. He got up and started back to the royal house, looking as he climbed at the shining black outlines of new beams and walls, just finished, and every part of Tara that he himself had restored from ruin and wilderness.

CHAPTER 3

The Feis of Tara

THE WASHED ROADS to Tara were empty the next morning. In many houses on the slopes of Tara people dressed quietly in their dark clothes, ate cold porridge, and then harnessed oxen to carts filled with straw cut from the late harvest. They went to a small rise behind the grove where the caretaker lifted bones down from their high lofts of stone or wood. Blackbirds watched from their perches in the yew trees, and by noon all the raised biers were empty. Small ingots of gold or copper were pressed into the care-taker's hands; his nails long and sharp for picking the flesh off the bones that the birds left.

At dusk carts began to move on the road to the Mound of the Hostages. Boys played the bodhran beside the track, as the people of Tara walked behind ox and cart, behind the bones of their dead that lay clean and white in the chaff for the bonfire. Through the new cut fields they walked in file, slowly with the sound of the bodhran, to the mound. Without speaking they watched the sky grow dark.

Then the men who waited for true dusk on the shore of Loch Dá Airbrech to the north and west drove a heavy chariot into the lake and swam again to the shore. When the horses reached deep water, the harness and iron traces pulled them down. As the sun disappeared at the far edge of the lake, they drowned.

In the grove of giant red-barked trees, as the last light of day fell between the trees into the clearing, Étaín waited for Eochaidh. She stood beside the well in the center of the clearing, a silver bowl with four gold horses on the rim beside her feet. She held a dried blossom of foxglove, the colour of her fleece cloak; her hair was braided and coiled in loops that touched her shoulders.

Eochaidh came toward her in his royal battle dress: a weapon belt, a purple cloak and a wide plaited gold torc that covered his chest. 'Woman, will I take you?'

She let a moment pass, watching his face, his eyes fixed on the druid behind her, the silence growing, his quick glance toward the hostages. She saw him look at her, wondering if she could possibly fail him, then meet her gaze, the question a flash of light in his eyes, and she answered him,

'It is for that I am here.
Since I have lived in this land,
Many men have wanted me,
But none has taken me.
It is you I have loved since I could speak;
You above all men that I desire.
I recognized you at once,
Eochaidh, High King.'

'Truth in the King
Is bright as the great wave's foam;
As the swan turning in sunlight;

As snow on the mountain.
A king's truth is power to overcome armies.
It brings milk into the world.
It brings corn and mast.'

'Let everyone see that she has not refused me,' said Eochaidh, in a loud voice, 'and that her bride price is satisfied.' He raised his hand, and horses were led into the edge of the clearing. 'Twenty mares,' he said, 'and seven female slaves.' Women came up and stood beside her.

Fedach said, 'If she will take him on the Mound of the Hostages, let all men call him High King. There before the hostages that he won by his own hand the King shall hear his geis that was found in waking vision by the druids of Ireland.'

Étaín crushed the foxglove between her hands and let it fall into the basin. She stirred the water with the rowan stick, whispering, 'Blend us; make us one to make new life.' And it came into her mind, 'Poison foxglove; perhaps he will die.' And then she sang,

'I am the blossom, the cup of foxglove,
The blood spilled and drunk;
The lamb and the she-wolf,
The mare and the stallion with the crushing hooves,
The cloud and the sky's fire.

I sing the salmon's song and the stream finds me.
I drink the wind and taste the eagle's kill.
I sleep on earth and the earth's seed grows within me.

You shake your mane, the waves break,
You leave the moon's print on grass and earth,

You move the sun and storm
Come now and change me.
Between the mare and myself make no division.

When you ride high above us, horse of sun,
Then I shall bear you children:
Kitten and cub, child and lamb, grass and flower.
And this I swear:
That I shall bear you horses,
Strong with shining coats and fierce eyes,
And there will be oats and corn and pasture forever
While I tend the earth.
You shall not starve
And no man shall raise his hand against you.'

Fedach said, 'Hear the song of the Sovereignty of Ireland! Now she serves him!' He was waiting for her to offer Eochaidh the bowl. She looked down and saw the remnants of the foxglove swirling, settling on the bottom.

Étaín made a cup of her hands, lifting the shining, dripping water from the surface of the bowl to Eochaidh to drink, as if he were an animal, and he drank from her hands.

'Bring the stallion to me,' she said quietly. Then she gave him the rowan stick. The women came up and led her to a chariot, and guards drove her out of the woods, back to the house to prepare for the Mound of the Hostages.

The moon was up when the royal chariot and the stallion were brought into the clearing. Eochaidh sat on the ground, his back against the well, shreds of red tree bark and moss clutched in his hands. He was covered with sweat although the night was cool; his hands shook. He felt weakness and nausea from the drink. There was a stabbing, pounding pain in his head, and he could see little, but he heard Fedach's voice.

'When you were born, you woke from your cloak of blood from the dreaming, sleeping dark and you found that you were alive. There was a mare and you were drawn to her out of your weakness and your fear, and she gave you drink. Now you are grown, a strong stallion. Go find her and ignite the stones between you.'

'I can't see,' whispered Eochaidh. 'I can't move.'

'All animals struggle to live. She'll be torn in half when she bears life for you.'

'Where are the hostages?'

'Gone to the Mound. Everyone is waiting.'

'Where is she?' he whispered.

'Take the harness. Look straight ahead, between the stallion's ears, and you will find your way. The track is open. You'll see the white mare. She's waiting.' He put the leather reins of the chariot harness in Eochaidh's hands and left him.

Eochaidh got up and walked slowly to the young stallion who had never drawn a chariot, who had run loose in Meath, claiming mares and the land for the king. Eochaidh laid the harness down on the ground. He rubbed his neck and back, talking low to him without pause, stroking his legs; touching every part of him that would feel the harness. When the horse stopped trembling and stood quietly for him, then he slipped the harness over his halter, still speaking softly, and fastened it.

He stepped into the chariot. A wave of nausea came over him, and he gripped the helm. He took a set of reins in each hand, and gently let the horse feel his hands through the leather. He saw the chieftains standing in the trees watching him, waiting for the horse to bolt. The stallion moved forward suddenly, then back, turning the chariot sideways; but the great wheels wrapped in straw did not go over.

The trees were close, and Eochaidh couldn't see the road out that led to the Mound. He struck the horse with his long whip, and he leapt forward. The chariot swung out and passed out of the grove between two trees, and it flew along the dark road to the Mound.

Seven women bathed Étaín in cold rainwater in the house while Eochaidh's guards stood outside. Étaín shook and her teeth chattered as they dried her, then rubbed her shoulders and her bare heels with gold. They dressed her in a cloak of soft white wool. They mixed gold with crushed malachite in a cupped stone, and drew around her eyes, crossing her cheekbones with the blue green marks, and gold.

'Once I put blue copper in the wound of Eochaidh's captain,' said one woman, as she laid the horsehair brush against Étaín's brow, 'with half his life poured out from it, and saw him rise and walk in two days from his deathbed, his wound clean and healed.' She drew a crescent under Étaín's eye. 'Your eyes are wells that can take poison from some evil look; the dust surrounds your eyes for protection,' she said.

'All brides are envied, more so the bride of Eochaidh, High King of Tara,' said the oldest woman, unbraiding Étaín's hair.

'Don't touch your eyes now; the dust burns,' said the first, wiping the brush on a clean cloth.

Now they worked quickly combing out the thick waves and her hair fell loose about her. 'She'll give them all a scare,' said the woman fastening the gold torc from Eochaidh around her neck, 'her face so young, painted like a beast; she doesn't look human now. Wicked. They'll be angry, maybe.'

'We've done nothing wrong; just what we were told,' said another, closing a belt around Étaín's cloak. 'Let Eochaidh be careful when he puts his hands on her, she's just a child.'

'No younger than you were when his brother had you.'

'What woman would go to him like that? No woman, a child maybe.'

'One who wanted to be rich,' said another, laughing.

'Be quiet,' said the woman closest to the door. 'His guards are all around the house. Is she ready?'

Outside, the guards' horses stood like dragons in the courtyard, their breath steam in the cold air. They bristled and danced close to the mare. She reared between two men, each pulling an end of the rope harness taut to keep her head down. Her mane was braided and each braid looped and tied off with narrow tethers of gold; her hooves were polished and shod with gold. The moon was covered by clouds and uncovered; the mare and the white stones around the house grew dim and bright again.

'She won't be ridden, not by a girl, not by me,' said the captain.

But then Étaín came out of the house, and they saw her eyes of a bird of prey, and her face of the bones of a horse's skull smoothed with gold, and her loose mane of gold. She touched the mare's chest, took up the lead and mounted, pressing her bare legs against the horse, turning towards the hill. The guards followed her.

She rode to the Mound along a small boreen. The hill grew lighter. Low clouds came down in a curtain, surrounding Tara, shutting out the land beyond. She could see the hostages standing on the top of the mound. The wind came like breakers against her, and she saw groups of faces and billowing cloaks and tents. They moved close and veered away, like the faces of curious fish that swim up and are suddenly gone; like ocean flowers that open and close, growing from rocks that slice and sting. The words they shouted were lost in the wind, sound deadened under water. The mare moved over shadowless ground, over heather drained of colour, kelp bleached in the wind.

She coiled a braid of mane around her fingers, struck the mare's haunches with her stick, and the horse went forward in a canter to the stone. The guards trailed off behind her, circling the hill.

She rode up among the hostages. The mare reared and the young boys backed away. All were richly dressed, with torcs and armlets of bronze or gold, but there were no weapons on them, and their ankles were bound in irons. There was one among them who seemed familiar, perhaps she had once seen him in her father's house. Beside that man Eochaidh's brother Ailill watched the crowd, his hand on his sword.

The hostages parted and Fedach came forward. Two white robed men followed him; they wore horse masks, one young with a yellow mane of wheat stalks, the other old with grey reeds for mane. Their hands were wrapped with cloth and copper wire, like hooves, and they had breasts of gilded bronze.

Fedach chanted,

'The strength of Lia Fáil is great.
The earth shakes, trees break and fall,
But Lia Fáil stands.

The one who climbs Lia Fáil,
Who brings a spark from stone,
The stallion's rub and thrust,
He is our father and our husband.
Who brings the joyful cry from stone,
He is the true king.

'If she takes him, he'll make new fire to kindle life in every beast and thing that grows; and the chiefs of Ireland will call him King.' He swung his staff close to the mare. She shied and tried to bolt. The hostage beside Ailill grabbed the bridle, and held the horse, and she quieted. He put his hand on Étaín's bare knee, saying, '*Bé Find*, don't be afraid.' Étaín shuddered, and cried out, 'Why do you call me that?'

He answered, 'It is your name, white lady,' and she thought again that she knew his face, but he turned away.

Then she chanted,

'I am Étaín Horse-Rider.
Between the mare and myself make no division;
And this I swear: I shall bear you strong children,
Foal and calf, grass and flower.
While I live you shall not starve.
Let no man raise his hand against another.'

There was the sound of thunder coming from the north; it was Eochaidh's chariot and she turned the horse to face the dark road.

Eochaidh saw a blur of people along the road as he passed, the huge wheels grinding the road beneath him, the feel of the axle in his legs, braced against the wind and the horse's speed. He must drive the chariot wheel against Lia Fáil, Fedach had told him. He saw the white stone ahead suddenly, and felt the horse fall out of a gallop. He took the reins in his left hand, and struck the stallion hard with the whip, and he lunged ahead.

He saw Étaín on the mare to the left of the stone, her white skin above the mare's white neck, and he drove the stallion hard towards her, swerving as the right chariot wheel met the stone with a screech like a beast slaughtered. The horses screamed. The wheel caught fire, its spokes wrapped with straw and agaric. It burned quickly. Étaín slipped down off the mare. Eochaidh touched a grass torch to the wheel, and lit the new fire below the mound. He cut the stallion free, and sent the empty chariot back down the hill.

People ran beside the chariot until it stopped, sputtering, in the grass, then put their sticks to the wheel to catch the fire. The women took their flares home to light the hearth-fires, and some hurled burning disks into the wet fields. The men came back and made a circle of torches in the road around Eochaidh's stallion.

He moved floating toward the white mare, his red mane and tail standing out straight, snorting and blowing. The mare ran before him, then stopped, swerved and kicked out, missing him. He struck her in the chest, turned, bit her side and she flew off again. She came fast to the edge of the crowd and guards stepped out of the line of torches with long whips, lashing her head and shoulders, leaving streaks of blood on her white sides. She screamed and turned and the stallion reared and struck out. She turned and ran again. When he caught and held her, and she was still for him, the crowd cheered, and Fedach on the mound called out above them, 'Eochaidh, hear your geis: Your doom will come when you give Étaín away.'

And in the dark Eochaidh took Étaín against the stone, his cloak around them both, and the wind was the sound of a terrible wave that broke against them; a great, destroying wave that turned the stones and the stars around and around, that spun out worlds and moons and wind and sea from the dark.

And when he let go of her, and they went down the hill, away from the mound where the hostages with their bright shields laughed and drank with Eochaidh's guards; away from the people walking to the feast with burning sticks saying they would never forget the cry that came from the stone Lia Fáil, the sure sign; when the mound was dark and empty again, the wind still roared.

CHAPTER 4

The Sickness of Ailill

IT WAS AT THE FEIS of Tara, when Eochaidh wed Étaín and took the sovereignty of Ireland, that the king's brother Ailill began slowly to die. No one guessed then how the shadows would grow under his eyes, his skin glowing pale, his limbs weak so that he couldn't walk alone; how he, who had been a warrior and horseman of great strength, would only whisper and clench his hands and tremble. The people of Tara and the royal hostages, and the chieftains and warriors who came to see the sacred marriage remembered the night well, but no one could say how Ailill got his sickness.

Only Ailill knew what the sickness was that was killing him, and at what moment it had shaken him as an eagle shakes a rat before she tears him open and devours him. It was when Étaín rode up the mound of the hostages, riding the white mare with her bare thighs gripping the horse, her loose hair streaming out behind her like a field of grass that the wind turns to water. It was her eyes, painted like a fierce bird of prey, watching them all, that shook him.

And then later, when she came into the banquet hall with Eochaidh and they sat across from him at the table, and everyone laughed and raised their glass in tribute; the marks of paint were gone, but a gold light came still from her washed face, her hair and her hands, like the sea at first light. There were faint bruises on her cheek and her neck above the gold torc that was too heavy for her. The perfect lines of her mouth were blurred. He saw that nothing was hidden; she had given herself to his brother and was changed.

To Ailill both were strangers who had shared some ordeal or conspiracy and grown close. He saw her narrow wrists poised above the polished table, her hands like cupped petals of white marsh orchids, like folded swan's wings as they rested at the table's edge. Then her eyes met his, dark blue and deep as a spear's cast, and he knew that she was his death, because he could not have her.

He listened to Eochaidh, smiled and turned the wine glass in his hand. He touched nothing on his plate. Although he didn't stare at Étaín, still he felt her on him, like a beast in the moment when a man knows that he won't be able to break free, or use his weapon, and that the beast won't let go of him until he's dead and devoured.

Later when everyone slept around the fire, full of wine and food, and Étaín slept in Eochaidh's arms, her back against his chest, and his rough hands buried in her white robe, Ailill couldn't sleep. He watched the sky lighten in the smoke hole over the hearth. When Étaín cried out in her sleep, and Eochaidh pulled her in to him close, then Ailill got up and went to his tent, but sleep would not come.

At daybreak he got up and walked to the tents of the hostages and spoke to the guards there. He passed the mound where a group of old women were breaking small round, nippled cakes and tossing the crumbs into the fire, saying 'This is for the fox, keep her from my chickens,' and he thought, 'That life is gone from me.' At the field where the white mare grazed among other mares again, girls laughed, counting the cuts on the horse, that the same number of months might bring them a husband. They ran away when they saw Ailill coming. He stood and watched the mare, cold with fear as if he were turning over the body of a fallen warrior, that it might be someone he knew and loved.

Eochaidh looked for him that day when the horse racing was about to start, but only later, when they had got to the jumping, when Étaín rode a grey stallion, did he see his brother, standing by himself at the other end of the course, watching. He didn't come to dinner that night, or join them at any other meal in the days that followed, and one day the guards reported to Eochaidh that Ailill had not met them at sunrise to give orders.

The king found him sitting alone in his tent, staring, his hands clenched into fists. The day was grey and dark, but there was no lamp burning in the tent. When he put his hand on his brother's shoulder, Ailill trembled.

'What's wrong? Do you have fever?' asked Eochaidh.

Ailill whispered, his voice flat, 'I can't leave the tent now.'

'Have you eaten bad food?'

Ailill shook his head. 'Forgive me for the trouble.'

'How long have you been ill? Ailill, are you in pain? You move like a man injured. I'll send Fedach to you. You'll have broth and wine. Now I'll find someone to take charge of the hostages.'

The food came back from the tent untouched. Fedach, who had cured Eochaidh's father of a festering boar's tusk wound with pine resins and thirty stitches, went to Ailill, then. He took Ailill's shaking hand in his own, and said, 'You must eat something, my lord.' He dipped a piece of bread in wine and gave it to him.

'I can't, the feel of it in my mouth sickens me,' whispered Ailill.

'Tell me why you can't eat. You make the king angry. What will I tell him?'

Ailill was silent.

'There are two things that can kill a man over which I have no power: love and jealousy. And for that you yourself must seek the cure.'

Every day afterwards Fedach went to Ailill's tent, and the scent of burning balsam and thyme was strong about him. The night came when Ailill couldn't raise himself from his bed, and the people of Tara knew it and that night they began to speak of plague. Fedach looked for the king.

He found Eochaidh alone in the banquet hall, sitting by the hearth, rubbing grease with a cloth into a new bridle. Fedach sat on a bench that faced the open door.

'He has no wound, no fever, nothing but weakness,' he said to Eochaidh. 'He'll die without some stroke of luck.'

'I have a hundred men who will do this work for me, bring me shining harness and blades, but I do it best myself. I trust no man more than Ailill to guard the hostages. And there is no doctor with skills beyond yours, Fedach. If you fail, Fedach, tell me the truth; how long will he live?'

'I don't think he's slept or eaten since Samhain, these thirty nights.' He sighed, and spoke with the heaviness of memory. 'I've seen a man fast against his enemy and die at his gate before twenty nights, and another, kept warm with blankets and wine, who breathed his last near sixty.'

'It's not a grudge fast; the sight of food sickens him. And no man who angered him lives.'

'He's strong; I've seen him pull an arrow out of his side and keep fighting.'

'You're not hiding plague from me?'

'He has none of the signs.'

'If you are sure you must say it; I've heard the talk. They say there's plague in Gaul, and my family trades outside the island. My brother must not die at Tara; that would be unlucky so soon after the feis. I don't want the hostages near him.' He stood up, pulling his cape around him. 'It's getting cold. The sun hardly moves. The solstice is nearly here, I must begin my circuit of the land. In six days I leave Tara to collect tribute, and I need Ailill beside me. The chieftains know him well. I had hoped you could send him with me.'

'There's nothing I can do, my lord.' Fedach stared at his hands.

'So you say. Of course you could be poisoning him yourself. But I'd hate to see your blood spilled in the snow this winter. You're an old man, Fedach, even for a druid, and you should die before me, easily, in your sleep. So I prefer to trust you.'

'Your father and his father did so,' said Fedach softly.

'I think they could afford to, not being High King.'

Fedach looked at him, and he saw that Eochaidh's face was changed, as clearly as a man putting on the mask of an animal. A slow trickle of ice entered him, and while Fedach kept his face and hands perfectly still, inside cold shock flooded him— that he had lived so long believing one thing, that his devotion to the tribe of Eochaidh was fast and his security complete, and that he was wrong.

Eochaidh said, 'I'll take Ailill and Étaín to Dun Fremain. She'll be safe there, caring for him. When he dies, she'll slaughter his cattle and bury him with all the rites, far from the hostages.'

Fedach stood. 'Then you must leave soon, lord.'

'What do you mean?'

'Every time I go to his tent, I'm afraid to see his corpse.'

'Keep him alive, Fedach, until Dun Fremain.' Eochaidh polished his sword. 'The hostages must see him alive. Make him eat; you can make a man do anything, if your means are persuasive.'

'Not if he has no will to live.'

Eochaidh looked up at him. 'Then he must be mad.'

'I can't tell.'

'Are you afraid of him?' he asked, smiling.

'He has no more strength in him now than a child.'

'Don't judge me, Fedach,' he said, fastening his sword to his belt. 'The loss will be great. But I must have tribute in my hands before he dies, or I am no King of Tara.'

'Then you must leave Tara tomorrow,' said Fedach, darkening his voice so that Eochaidh wouldn't hear his hope.

'I will. Go now, prepare Ailill to ride to Dun Fremain. You will accompany him. I'll be glad to go home; Tara is no hospitable place for any but the dead.'

CHAPTER 5

The Drive to Dun Fremain

TO THE CHILDREN of Meath it seemed that the sun itself went out of Tara that next day. At dawn they watched the road that led west to Dun Fremain, to Uisnech and Cruachan in Connaught and the western sea. First came Eochaidh, Étaín beside him. Ailill came next and a hundred guards followed, all mounted, and then the cattle, slaves, goldsmiths, musicians and carts carrying chests of clothing and treasure, and a hundred warriors after.

As the sun rose it glared from every pool of standing water in the road, and from the gold breastplate of the king's red horse, and from the king's neck, and Étaín's forehead, and from the chest of the king's brother.

When they reached the place where the road became overgrown, and the walls of the fort at last disappeared beyond a low hill, Eochaidh gave the signal to halt. A cart filled with sheepskins was brought to the front of the procession, and Ailill was helped from his horse, and laid in the cart. Then they started again, making their slow way to Dun Fremain.

The road to the west led across the esker mounds, low hills of sand and rock that rose above the stunted bare-limbed oak forests and the bog. The land was flat and dark, the sun stuck low in the sky; before the company had ridden long it began to sink again. At dusk Eochaidh gave orders to camp in the lee of a ridge of bog, and build a fire. While there was still light they moved the carts onto the ridge, to block the hard wind. They ate dried beef and sweet oat cakes, and the women brought Étaín blankets and mulled wine.

Eochaidh came up behind Étaín, standing close; one hand on her thigh, the other moving her hair from her neck, he kissed her bare shoulder. His beard was wet with mead. He took her to his own bed beside the fire, where Ailill lay on his side, staring. Beyond the smoke of the fire warriors drank hot mead and laughed.

When Eochaidh went off to speak with his captain, Étaín waited for him, standing on his bed. She held her blanket close against the freezing wind, her eyes tearing from the smoke, looking at the rough dark hills all around. Eochaidh's guards and slaves walked past slowly, staring at her.

When Eochaidh came back, he set a cup of hot poteen down at Ailill's shoulder. He took off his cloak and pulled Étaín down under the skin blanket. He lay still for a moment, one hand on her, touching her breast through the wool, watching the sky. Then he pulled the clothes off her and his hands were cold on her skin.

When Eochaidh made love to her she knew that his men would not look, and when she opened her eyes she always saw Ailill's back turned toward them. He lay close by, nearly an arm's reach away from their bed. She saw that the cup of liquor had spilled.

Afterwards, when Eochaidh slept, she lay on her back, hearing Ailill breathing fast and shallow, his back still toward her. She wondered what kept him alive, the only brother of Eochaidh that everyone feared. Then she didn't hear his breath. She didn't want to move in her bed because Eochaidh was a light sleeper, and if she woke him he would desire her again before he slept, but the idea would not leave her that perhaps Ailill was dead. If Ailill died now they would bury him in the bog and Eochaidh would take her with him on his circuit of the land. If he lived only two or three days more Eochaidh would leave her in Dun Fremain; perhaps for one year he would leave her alone while he was feasted in the royal forts of Ireland. And the only thing that could keep her from crying out when Eochaidh touched her and drove all his anger into her was the hope of an empty fort above a lake and guards who would care nothing for her, and let her walk alone. But she could not hear Ailill breathe, even though the wind had dropped.

Then from some ridge a moan began, a distant keening that rose and fell, one voice of low timbre and great sweetness. Each note was sung out on a long breath, the pitch and strength falling as the breath failed, then another note begun out of the silence, held and strengthened but never passing a certain boundary of solemn restraint, falling and dying, and begun again. It seemed that each note was picked out of the night as one star might be chosen, as if the song was a signal to one star. And Étaín, who had first gone cold at the sound, thought, if this is the keen for Ailill, so be it.

Ailill moved. He turned his head towards her. His lips moved, and he spoke. 'A wolf. Don't be afraid; he won't come to the fire.' She smiled and nodded to him. He closed his eyes and turned his face toward the sky. She saw his breath misted in the air above him.

The stars moved and it got colder on the ridge where Eochaidh's party camped, but Étaín didn't sleep. The wolf did not sing again, but when she turned, as Eochaidh turned in his sleep, his arm around her waist and his knees pressed behind her knees, she saw Ailill looking at her. She didn't move the hair away that had fallen over her face, but closed her eyes.

When the rim of the world was ringed with light, and the hills began to lighten, then all through the camp people woke. Women brought turf to the fire, and Étaín saw the hard looks they gave her, still warm in her bed, with Eochaidh's arm lying across her throat and his breath on her face. The horses nickered and called for their grain. Eochaidh got up from his bed, and stretched, naked. He put on his weapon belt, fastened his long knife, threw his cloak over him and went off to feed them. Soon after she heard a boy's frightened pleading, then Eochaidh's voice, angry, rising above the boy's screams, then silence. When they left the ridge Étaín rode past the body of the boy, his face beaten. She saw Eochaidh's raw hands and his knuckles split. During the night the boy had fallen asleep, and horses had been lost.

As Ailill was laid into the cart, Fedach saw his bright cheeks, and he rode up to Eochaidh at the front of the procession. 'I can't be sure that Ailill will live until tomorrow night.'

Eochaidh said, 'We'll ride hard to Dun Fremain.'

'If we go any faster, it will be too hard for him. The cart going over this rough land will kill him.'

'Don't give me riddles to solve this morning, Fedach. If you see death's mark on him, then we won't walk to Dun

Fremain. I've ridden with four hundred warriors from Dun Fremain at mid-winter, and seen the sun set on Tara's walls that same day. These horses are fit, the cart won't fall apart; you'll keep his body alive until we reach the lake, or I will lay you out together in the bogs and the wolves will eat you. It'll be a hard winter if they're hunting out of the forests now; the boy said he saw one running along the hill. Now he is making a feast of my red mare, and I'd rather see him eat an old man than my horse.'

'There is nothing I can do to keep him alive, lord.'

Eochaidh stared at Fedach. Then he turned to Étaín, taking the small poteen flask from his belt and putting it in her hand. 'Go, Étaín, and give this to my brother, so that he won't feel the hard ride. Ailill has never refused my flask. Perhaps he hasn't drunk these weeks because he feared poison. He's your brother now, Étaín, care for him. It's you who will bury him, but not this day.'

Étaín turned her mare, broke out of line and cantered back to Ailill's cart. Guards took her horse while she swept up her cloak with one hand, and crawled up into the cart. Ailill lay back in the sheepskins, his eyes sparkling with fever. Étaín leaned over him. He looked like Eochaidh, despite his dark hair and blue eyes, but the skin of his face across his bones was like a bodhran stretched too tight, that will burst in a dry wind. His dark beard was thin, the bones of his broad shoulders sharp beneath his cloak. He stared at her. Étaín showed him Eochaidh's flask. 'This is no poison. Drink this, Ailill, please drink it.' She wiped away tears from her face, put one hand gently against his chest and said, 'Ailill, I swear by the gods my people swear by, I want you to live.'

She lifted his head with her hand, and raised the flask to his lips, and he drank. Fedach and the guards who had been standing by the cart left. When the poteen made him sleep she covered him with blankets, and made a shield of skins to keep the wind off from him.

All that day she rode beside him in the cart, keeping her hand on him, and Eochaidh drove them in a steady canter to Dun Fremain. There was still light in the sky when they came upon Eochaidh's herd, the calves scattering before them, as they followed the shore of the Cold Lake below the fort. The cattle had cleared the woods all the way down to the lake, and the trees had lost their leaves, so that the water glowed red through the bare birch and rowan.

She saw the shape of Fremain Hill ahead, a perfect cone, rising dark and high above them. They followed the boreen slowly uphill, around and around the steep sides, Étaín guiding the cart past rocks and holes. She watched Ailill sleep, and eyed the peak of the hill above her to the right or left, coming closer, until finally the walls of the fort appeared. The gates of the fort were opened for them, and in the courtyard there were torches beside the stables and the great house. Men carried Ailill into the house, and Étaín followed them down a corridor and into a large room that looked out on a dark field.

Soon after Eochaidh came into the room. He stood by the bed, frowning, staring down at his brother. 'He looks dead.'

'He is not,' said Étaín. She pulled the gold torc off her neck and held it under Ailill's lips. A fine mist blurred the gold. 'See? He lives.'

Eochaidh shook his head. 'More dead than alive. Well then, I leave tomorrow. Stay with him tonight, Étaín. I've sent riders back to Tara and ahead to Slanemore saying that all is well. Ailill lives; it's no lie.

'When he's dead and buried you'll come to me, Étaín. I'll send back messengers from every camp and fort; you'll know where I sleep. Now I'll show you where you will bury him.'

They went together down the hallway and out into the courtyard. It was raining. She followed him to a high gate in the rampart that looked north. It was heavy with rain and swung out slowly. Below the rampart the land was terraced, then dropped off. There were small mounds at the edge of the drop, like the blunt paws of a beast grasping the cliff.

'These are the graves of my kin. Feast him ten days when he's gone. You must slaughter his cattle too. He has five or six hundred cows, and as many calves; the cows are marked with copper rings. You yourself kill the first calf, then let the butchers finish them. When you come bring me some of that meat, Étaín.' He put his hands under her cloak, and pulled her to him. 'I'm tired,' he said, rubbing his face against her neck. 'I could sleep in Dun Fremain. I can't sleep in another man's house. I'll rest better when you come, Étaín.' He pulled the hood up over her wet hair. 'Winter is on us. Go back now to Ailill. I'll come to his room in the morning before I leave.'

Étaín sat that night in a chair beside Ailill's bed. She gave him sips of water, and kept the blankets on him. All night it rained, and made a drum of the roof. She closed her eyes and sometimes the drum would be farther away as the rain lessened, and she willed it to stop, so Eochaidh could leave early and travel far the next day before his brother died.

Then she was afraid that he might die, as weak children and animals do in deep sleep, in the time of deepest cold before dawn, and she sat close to him, watching his chest rise and fall. His arms and legs were tense as if he waited for some blow. She put one hand on his shoulder and the other on his face, stroking his cheek lightly as she would stroke a horse. She talked to him about Inber Cichmaine, about the salt marshes and the secret lair of the kingfisher and his strange way of stabbing fish out of the river, and about the salmon leaping up the stones. She sang songs that her father taught her, and that she and her cousins had invented while they made forts in the reeds at the riverbank. He said nothing, but his eyes followed her. She couldn't read them; they were dark and soft from pain, or weakness, as a warrior who has bled too much. But when she gave him water, and he put his shaking hand up to guide the flask, his hand moved past the skin bag, and stopped beside her cheek. He took a strand of her gold hair between his thumb and finger, twisting it in the lamplight. He whispered, 'Lovely anyone until Étaín. Beautiful anyone until Étaín.'

So Eochaidh found her near dawn, with her hand on his brother's chest, and two guards beside the door, and Ailill was still alive. He set down a small boat of pure gold on the table beside the bed. The boat was the size of his hand, with oars as fine as sparrows' bones. 'I made it for him,' he said, his voice husky with sleep. 'Put it in his grave.'

'I will,' she said, and was silent, waiting for him to speak again.

But Eochaidh only stared at the window, and falling rain; then he turned and left the room.

When the last shouts and the clatter of harness and weapons faded from the window, Étaín sent for bread from the kitchen. Ailill took small pieces from her hand. She left him with the guards and walked down the hall, finding the room that held her trunks and blankets. She washed her face in a copper cauldron, put on a heavy cloak and went outside.

The rain had stopped. The courtyard was empty except for a big dog who was drinking from a pond of rainwater that had spread over the stones. He sat down and cocked his head, seeing his reflection. The rain began again and the pond was mottled silver, a breathing salmon. She called the dog and he followed her out of the courtyard.

The upper terrace followed the curve of the hill north, leading to a steep path that went up into a stand of ash and oak. The crest of Fremain Hill was hidden in the grove. Étaín took the path. Here the grass was ungrazed, thick and long; halfway up the lake appeared, filling the land below. The clouds were thinning, and the sun hung low above the distant shore, although it was near midday. Étaín pulled the new growth from a branch of pine. The dog came up beside her. 'Are you Eochaidh's dog? Has he left you behind?' He followed her down the hill, and ran off as she went into the house.

That night the scent of pine needles filled the house, and Ailill had red broth with thyme and tarragon. Étaín had a bed brought into Ailill's room, so she could stay beside him all night. One night she couldn't sleep, and it was late when she got up from the bed and stood at the window, singing softly,

One winter's night
The golden ball went down the well.
Who shall retrieve it?
'Not I,' said the bear, 'I'm sleeping.
I won't burn my paws, my beautiful sharp claws.
Not I.'
Branches, bones, sharpen the blades.

Roll wheel, come back sun.
Who shall retrieve it?

'Not I,' said the stag, 'With my seven tines,
I won't scorch my crown.
Not I.'
Branches, bones, sharpen the blades.
Shadows growing, day is falling.
We are so cold.
Roll wheel, come back sun.
Who shall retrieve it?

'I,' said the serpent in the well,
As she coiled around the gold.
'Let it burn and crack.
I'll shed my skin.
Here is your gold.'
Roll wheel, come back sun.

She turned to the bed where Ailill lay, and saw that he
was watching her. 'Ailill, you must sleep; every man must
sleep and live.' She sat on the edge of his bed, beside him.

'Perhaps if you tell me the cause of your pain, you'll
grow strong again.'

He shook his head.

'There's nothing so terrible that it can't be told. I've
brought pine into the house, Ailill; if you sleep the scent of
the needles will take away your shame. But you must sleep.
Ailill,' she said, 'you look at me without stopping.'

'I can't help it.'

'You're better now than you were. I thought you were
going to die. Perhaps you will live, Ailill. Do you want to
live?'

He said nothing.

'Ailill, will you tell me the cause of your illness?'

'It is love of you,' he answered.

'Then I'm sorry that you've been so long in telling it.' She spoke quietly. 'If I had known it, you would have been healed before this.'

As the solstice drew near, and the sun slowed to standstill along the horizon, it seemed that Ailill improved. His hands grew steady, and strength began to come back into him. But still shadows lay beneath his eyes, and he did not sleep.

When the solstice was four nights off a rider came from Eochaidh in the Wicklow mountains. He brought gifts for Étaín, amethyst cups, and gold bracelets, and word that he would stop in Dun Fremain before he went south again.

That night Étaín woke suddenly, and saw Ailill standing above her.

'What is it? You frightened me.'

He said nothing, looking down at her. Étaín got up and took his arm to lead him to his bed.

'Don't,' he whispered. 'Étaín, I can't bear your touch. Your touch burns.'

She let him go.

'Étaín, if you desire it, then I will be healed.'

'I desire it.'

'I haven't slept since I saw you. Awake, I dream of your eyes and hair, of your skin. Soon Eochaidh will come back, and hating him I must never touch you, never speak of you. Étaín, tell me what to do.'

He knelt down at her feet. She put her hand on his hair, and saw how much silver had come into it since Samhain, since she had become the wife of Eochaidh. She raised him up, and he put his arms around her, and held her close. She felt no fear of him. Her arms went around him slowly, touching his back, his shoulder, and she thought, 'These are the bones that I was to lay in the earth. But he lives; he is strong.'

'Étaín, make love to me and I'll be well again. I'm not a man until you love me,' he said. 'Let me sleep. Let me be free of you.'

'I will,' she whispered, 'but not in his house, not here.'

A sob came from him; she held him until he was quiet.

'In the grove above the fort,' whispered Étaín, her cheek against his shoulder. 'I'll meet you there in the third hour before dawn. Ailill, you don't betray him. Go to sleep now,' she said, stepping away from him. Then she went out of his room, and down the cold hallway to her own room; but she did not sleep.

CHAPTER 6

The Tryst

IT WAS STILL DARK when Étaín left the fort. She crossed the wet grass instead of taking the path from the terrace, because the path was made of white stones, bright in the moonlight, and guards watched from the rath. The dog came with her; he ran back and forth ahead of her, hunting, as she climbed to the grove. At the edge of the woods he disappeared into a hazel thicket, and when the thicket was still again she couldn't hear him at all.

There was a small clearing ahead in the middle of the grove, but not until she walked into it did she see the man in the dark cloak sitting on the stump, with his back to her.

The man stood and turned to her, and as he came toward her she thought, this is not Ailill, this is a stranger. But when he reached her, and looked at her, she knew him. He kissed her suddenly, without warning. She didn't know how he moved to her, or met her lips, but his mouth touched hers with perfect pressure, strength and gentleness, and when he moved away, the feel of it remained, and went through her.

His voice went through her like the bodhran, low and resonant; and his eyes, blue green under black brows, were sad. He asked her if she was well, and to Étaín it seemed as if she had stepped off the hill and been caught, and that it would be a grave trespass of faith to ask if she would fall. And the feel of his mouth on hers remained.

He took her hands in his, and looked at her face, saying, 'Étaín' and then laughing. 'Ah...you are so beautiful. Come, look at the lake,' and they walked through the grove to the edge of the hill. The lake was black and broken with waves. 'Étaín, tell me about the river; about the salt marsh, and how you played there and swam through the reeds.'

'It was forbidden. My father –'

'– he wouldn't let you? Why?'

'I don't remember. My parents were old when I was born. They had no other children. But I was careful; I knew the tides. I remember the frogs and the owls hunting.'

'Were you lonely?'

'I don't know. There's no answer. Were you?'

'Sometimes; there was someone I had lost. But I liked to walk alone.'

'By the Cold Lake.'

'Yes, by the lake,' he answered, kissing her.

'It's beautiful now,' said Étaín. 'So dark and rough.'

'A long time ago there were two swans that came every year, and one day I didn't know the eggs had hatched, and swam too close. They rose up out of the water, striking, like stallions, and chased me.'

'On Inber Cichmaine they come every winter.'

'They will, unless death parts them.'

'How can they find their way?' she whispered.

He stared at her, then said slowly, holding her close to him. 'How does the sun find its way back along the rim of the world? Every year they fly to Slievenamon, when the sun's beam falls into the Mound of the Hostages.'

She was suddenly still. 'I would go there,' she said softly, her arms around his neck, her face against his shoulder. 'I want to see them.'

He pulled back from her, taking her hands. 'I won't speak of that place.'

'Eochaidh is far away.'

'I know it. You're cold.' He put his cloak around her. 'Winter is here; the solstice very near.' They walked back to the bench. He put his foot against a log, and a chunk of rotten wood crumbled and fell away. 'Étaín, do you know the marsh piper's song?'

'Where the swans sleep, you sing,
Your throat chipped from oak.
Here the ducks mutter and slip
On the tides and eddies of the Log King.

Here is silver and gold
For the marsh leeches
Camped in their mud keeps.
They wait for the battle that never comes.

The Log King keeps his secret;
One day he'll drift away, worm-eaten.
No procession to his drowning pond,
The King is dead; your song begins.

Now the swans stir from their mound of grass.
To the hill of the moon you fly,
Your song like an arrow lies
At the feet of the giantess.'

After a moment he said, 'He has drifted away.'

'He must not die, Ailill.'

'He'll rot as all men. Shouldn't we have happiness?'

'There can be no peace after, Ailill. You must keep Eochaidh safe, as I have kept you.'

'I have done so all his life, but from this time out, I cannot.'

'Don't speak of it,' she said, touching his mouth with her hand. His black beard was streaked with silver, but his eyebrows were completely black. He looked down at her and smiled.

'Where is Slievenamon, the hill of the moon?' she asked, looking away.

'A long way off, Étaín, but you will see it.'

'What is it?' she whispered, her head under his chin.

'The furze burns on the mountain all summer long through the mist, and cuckoos sing. The stones are blood red, small and cold, like the hearts of birds. There is a bed of swan's down, and you will dream there, and men will do what you dream.' He touched her face, 'Étaín, I can't make love to you. There's no strength in me, I'm ashamed. Leave me now, before it's light.'

She walked down the hill alone and went into the fort, to her room.

At midday Étaín was sitting in the courtyard when Ailill came to her.

'Forgive me, Étaín,' he said, 'but I fell asleep, waiting, and woke just now. Did you wait long for me?'

'I brought breakfast to your room, but couldn't wake you,' said Étaín, smiling. 'It's good that you have slept, Ailill.' She touched his hand. 'I'm glad to see you so well. I'll meet you tonight at the same hour.'

'I won't fail you,' he said, and went back into the house.

That night Étaín went again to the wood on the hill above the fort, and she found him there, waiting for her, looking down at the lake.

'See how the swans move,' he said. 'They keep a perfect distance, drifting. This wooing is cautious, but they are of one mind.' He turned to her and kissed her, and she stood looking at him, her hands on his shoulders.

'I won't lose you, Étaín; you are marked as surely as this ground, or the wolf's song that will bring him back to her side.' He kissed her mouth, her jaw, her eyes.

'There's no shame in it,' she whispered. 'You are worthy to be High King of Tara.'

'Still I'm afraid to let go of you, even this night,' he said, holding her close. 'I am afraid...' he said, stroking her face gently with his hands. 'Étaín, now I must go away, but will you stay with me tomorrow night, the longest night of the year, until sunrise?'

'I will come,' she said and she left him in the grove.

The next day Ailill passed Étaín in the corridor, and he said, 'Tonight, I won't sleep.' Then he went to his room, and he built a fire. He kept it going all evening, and bathed his face in cold water to stay awake. But before the hour of tryst, he fell asleep.

In her room Étaín put on a tunic of green silk, embroidered with gold leaves and flowers along the hem and across the shoulders, and over that she fastened a purple cloak of soft fleece. She let the fire die in her room, and when the hour of tryst came, she went out of the house. The grove was pale with mist. He was standing under a fir tree, beside two dark grey horses tethered there.

'Étaín,' he said, coming to her, and taking her hands, 'Étaín Echraide.'

'Why do you call me that?'

'You wear the colors of your captivity, Étaín,' he said, his voice shaking.

'I don't understand you.'

'Étaín, ride with me tonight, the longest night of the year. I'll show you where my family watched the sun rise at solstice long ago. Do this last for me and then if you wish it, I'll leave you in peace.'

They rode down the hill out of the mist, north and west, past the narrow lake of iron and the lake of the glen, a long cantering ride over the bogs. But the horses didn't tire, and the night was mild. The sky cleared over a hill that stood alone on the plain, and they rode through the pine forest that covered the rim of the mountain.

'What is this place called?' asked Étaín.

'Brí Léith,' he said.

'Is there a house?'

'There is.'

'Does someone live there now?'

He reached over and took the reins, and the horses stopped. He got down and lifted her off the horse, and held her apart from him.

'Étaín, do you not know me?'

She pulled away from him. 'Know you? Of course, Ailill, I know you,' but even as she spoke, looking at him, at his eyes, she began to see that perhaps he was not Ailill, and she became afraid. It seemed that she must be mad, and that everything was false. Perhaps even her marriage had been arranged in secret, long planned by Eochaidh and her father for some terrible hidden purpose. She had torn the veil of the lie; and she would go mad, begin to scream and never stop until she was dead, the world shattered, if she could not repair it, and forget what she had seen.

'I am your husband, Étaín,' he said.

'That can't be.'

'I am, Étaín.'

'Who are you?' she whispered.

'I am Midhir. I have loved you for a thousand years, and you were taken from me, and now I have found you again. Why was the river dangerous? Why was it forbidden? I was the rider, Étaín. I nearly took you then, but you were a child. Still I could have kept you from Tara. Remember; you are Étaín Echraide; and I was blind; it's you that healed me in the cave of the Brugh, on the longest night, like this night.

'It is she that was sung of in the land.
It is she the king is seeking.
Once she was called Bé Find,
Now she is our Étaín.'

'You are my husband's brother, and your illness has touched your mind. We must go back to Dun Fremain now.'

Then he put one hand on her face, gently, and raised his cape over her, and Étaín saw moonlight go through it, and she saw the purple veins of great wings. He held a staff of quartz, and his voice was like a wave of the sea breaking against her, and she couldn't breathe, as if she were underwater. 'Étaín Echraide, you must know me,' he said, and his hair was gold, and he wore a tunic of black wool with gold spirals in the hem.

She said, 'I am dreaming now. I don't know this place.'

'It's no dream, Étaín. Walk with me.'

She followed him up an overgrown trail, with nettles and thorns catching her cloak. They came to a stream, and a ruined hearth where a small house had once been.

'There's no madness in you, Étaín. Nothing that lives can be destroyed. My father the Daghda could make a storm or end one without thinking; his will was one with weather. And I once watched you by the salt marshes, and willed that time would bring us safe together.'

'How can I believe this?'

'Étaín, you had this way about you once; what some call magic; you have it still. There are few now that live as we; and I am one of the last. But here is another proof: it was I that made Ailill fall in love with you, so that his longing for you brought him close to death, and only you could heal him. And now his desire for you is gone, and he is himself again. At Dun Fremain you will believe me. But walk with me now to the house.'

They came out of the forest, then, and Étaín saw a ruined rath with quartz stones lying in the heather below, and beyond the fort, a house still standing. Midhir pushed open the heavy door, and stood aside to let her pass.

There was a narrow hallway, and many small rooms led off the passage, each with an arched threshold, elaborately carved as interlacing vines, flowers, and shells, that led on to other rooms, with four steps up or down; all carved, small and dark in spite of the lamps. There were carved benches and couches in alcoves, and where the walls were not carved they were painted or hung with tapestries, woven with the images of animals and lakes and sea in rich colours. In one room there was a carved boat with linen sails stretched over it, and deep mattresses of down and soft blankets in it for sleeping; and there were hearths and amber lamps of burning oil in every room. There were no windows, but the house was not confining; it was close and deep and safe like a grove of old trees.

They climbed the staircase that wound upwards like the spine of a shell, and stood in a long hall with a cold hearth, skylights and the muttering of hawks. And it seemed quiet and deserted to Étaín, as if the hall just had been full of voices and smoke, and now the banquet had been cleared away and the people gone.

'Do you remember, Étaín?' he asked. 'Like a trick. I am cruel,' he said. 'Come outside with me, then, and I'll show you the land.'

They sat on the rampart, looking down over the forest, with the flat bogland stretched out below. He looked at her solemnly, saying,

'Étaín, will you come with me now
To Slievenamon, hill of the moon,
That land where peace is?
There is neither mine nor thine;
No hunger, or sickness,
There death cannot come.
There teeth are white, dark the brows,
The body smooth and bright as snow,
Hair like the crown of the primrose,
On every cheek the scarlet foxglove.
Warm sweet streams flow through the land
Of mead and wine.
Oh Woman of Light, Bé Find,
If you come with me, to my people,
A crown of gold shall be on your head.
Honey, wine, ale, fresh milk
You will have with me.
There in the mist we are safe, Bé Find.

We see everyone on every side
And no one sees us.
But if you do not come
That place will be a land of desolation.
War shall be on Eochaidh,
Battle against many thousands,
And the Brugh shall be destroyed.'

He took her hand, and in silence they looked out over the dark plain, and an eagle floated down into the pines. Then Étaín answered him, her voice low.

'It is my death and yours you're asking. I can't go with you. You are a stranger to me, and I am bound to Eochaidh. If he will let me go...if he will let me...then I'll come with you. But more than that I cannot give. I remember a man with gold hair and eyes like yours, by the salt marsh. But the rest is dream, and one who believes dreams may be deceived.'

'Do you hate me now, Étaín?' he asked.

She said, 'I do not. But you are terrible to me, and I can't love you.'

'Then I will come again.' He moved to her. 'Watch for me at Tara.' He kissed her, and it was again a sudden cast of spear, the target perfectly met.

She was standing alone on the hill above Dun Fremain.

In the east the sun broke over the lake. Below her, a reddish gold light moved across the cairns, warming the stones. And she sang,

'He is gone, gone from me and I am lost.
Cry like a calf from its mother parted,
Breaking the field's peace.
No comfort, but him against me.

He is gone; what shall I do?
How live one hour out of his company?
And now the sun turns back.
Each day grows longer,
More full of sorrow that he is gone from me.

See how the sun falls upon the graves below,
A terrible glow,
And he, too, could die, out of my company
While I chose not to keep him safe beside me.

Let the sun go dark.
Snow, hide these graves,
The trampled grass where he walked beside me.
Make my heart white and cold against him

Now it is Eochaidh who is coming,
Eochaidh I will watch for;
And I will be myrrh and balm for his secrets,
And protect him; my husband, my king.'

She stayed on the hill until dawn passed into the long
dusk, and it snowed on Dun Fremain, and covered the
mounds of Eochaidh's dead, and the path leading down to
the fort. And she stood in the snow and filled her hands
with snowflakes, and watched speckled starlings. The bare
branches of the rowan, and the oak, with its dead leaves,
filled with snow. She called the dog, but he didn't come.
She went at last into the house.

As she passed Ailill's room the door opened, and a dark-
haired girl stepped out, with her hand on the door, her back

to the hall. She turned, seeing Étaín. 'Here is your brother's strange bride to visit you, Ailill,' she said, laughing, and ran down the hall.

Ailill came to the door, tying his cloak at the chest and waist. He said, 'You see, Étaín, I am completely healed,' and laughed. 'Eochaidh's wife is pure gold,' he said, touching her hair, 'and of such loyalty to him that she would betray him to save his only brother. Such devotion must be rewarded; he'll be grateful to see me well. But the rest is our secret. You're pale as ice. Étaín, have you waited all night and day for me in the snow? But you are safe now.'

After that meeting it seemed to Étaín that he avoided her, and when they met at dinner in the hall he rarely spoke to her, but talked and laughed with the guards. Eochaidh came to Dun Fremain and it was near mid-summer when they drove their cattle across the plains to Tara. The furze was blazing gold along the rough track, and they made camp by the old marks of bonfire, and the bones of the stable boy, clean and white in the heather. Eochaidh put Étaín between himself and Ailill that night for warmth, and the brothers drank poteen and told stories of battle far into the night.

A feast was held in Tara to welcome Eochaidh. Night after night his warriors crowded the hall, drinking, feasting, and fighting. A young girl from a settlement below the hill was raped and when her father went to the fort to demand justice, his body was found the next day on the dung heap behind the stables. Then four guards were burned alive in their tent, and afterwards a guard was placed in every farmer's house to watch the man, and women brought the cows home early to the byre, and kept their children beside them.

The hostages and the warriors thrived on the people's milk and cheese, and the king's horses grazed their winter fields. Still they said that it was Eochaidh and his thousand warriors who kept Tara strong, and that any who spoke against him wished their own sons to die. That summer the roads became overgrown, and the poets did not stop in Tara, although it was their right to cross boundaries and seek protection in every house so that the people would know the truth of things that passed in the land.

BOOK IV – WAR

CHAPTER 1

Fidchell

IT WAS SAID in Tara that Eochaidh had never lost a game of fidchell. He would challenge any man, and when he was tired of the company of his guards, he would ride to the Queen's Bed and play fidchell with Étaín. She always knew when he was coming; when the crows left the roof, and the tame fowl screeched and ran to their nests in the byre, she would take the gold fidchell pieces out of their chest, and lay them out on the gaming table of black and white squares. She would be waiting for him when he ducked under the threshold and took his chair at the table. He always drank a cup of milk from the red cow in her byre, and thanked the servant who took his cup away.

It was no secret that Étaín had bad dreams; her screams had woken many in Tara. She would lie uncovered in the cold to keep sleep from her, lying still with her eyes closed, but at the edge of sleep the shape of a beast or blood came to her, and she would start awake, screaming, feeling Eochaidh's hands on her, shaking her, her eyes open but still seeing the dream.

When Eochaidh left his bed she often went to the wood of giant red-barked trees, and lay down in the deep bed of bark and needles. Before the sun passed the hill of Tara and entered the forest she would go to her house and wait for him. But one long summer day she watched the light move about the forest floor, making a patch of moss bright, or a tangle of briars where a sparrow searched in the dim sharp recesses for seeds. Near dusk deer crossed the ravine, and foxes; beetles climbed over pieces of bark beside her still hand. Then hundreds of snails came out around her, no larger than the nail on her smallest finger, with striped shells of brilliant yellow, green, coral, and violet. The many different colours were beyond counting.

When she entered the dark house, Eochaidh rose from his chair, great in that low room as a giant tree with its crown against the fog. He hadn't touched the cup of milk beside him. She saw that her cloak was stained with moss and pitch, and her loose hair matted with burrs and needles. Her servants ran quickly to bring her a clean robe, but Eochaidh took her and began to strip the clothes from her himself, and the servants and guards left the house.

No man had ever taken a woman in that place before, as it had been forbidden in all memory. But that night Eochaidh laughed from her bed at the leering, squatting goddess carved in the beam above the door. The next day he ridiculed the geasa of the High Kings, asking Fedach how harm could come to a land if a king didn't rise sunwise from his sleep; and he ordered his men to cut down the grove of red-barked trees that was the last of their kind and make new roof beams for his banquet hall.

On the morning of the equinox, Eochaidh rose early and climbed the rampart of Tara to look out over his land. The oaks were turning gold in the forest beyond the fields, where the road to the west disappeared under their branches. When he turned around he found a warrior he didn't know standing with his back to the sun watching him.

The man carried a five-pointed bronze spear in his hand, and a shield of silver that would crack at the first thrust of an iron sword. He wore a king's tunic of scarlet edged with gold, and his hair was gold. A huge red dappled stallion pawed the ground beside him.

Eochaidh put his hand on his sword hilt easily as the stranger stepped forward, saluting him.

'Welcome, warrior,' said Eochaidh. 'You're standing before the sun; I can't see your face.'

The man turned. His eyes were blue-green, with fine scars out from his left eye, like the rays of the sun. This stranger had not been in Tara last night, and all the gates of the fort were still closed and guarded at this hour. Guards were posted on every road, watching the sea road from the east, the Laigin road south, and the west road to Cruachan and the armies of Connaught.

'I know you,' the man announced. 'The High King of Tara is known to everyone.' He stepped forward, putting the reins of his horse in Eochaidh's hand. 'For the stables of Tara,' he said.

'What is your name?' asked Eochaidh.

'Not famous. I am Midhir of Brí Léith. I've come to play fidchell with you.'

'You are welcome, then,' said Eochaidh. 'I know that place, north of my stronghold Dun Fremain. It's nothing but bog and waste.' He pointed to Midhir's stallion. 'Where do you hide the rich fields that he has grazed on?' He signalled his guards; they came down the rampart and took the horse away. 'The fidchell table is in my wife's room, and she is still asleep,' he said.

'Do not wake Étaín,' said Midhir. He stared at Eochaidh's body, at the places on the neck and chest and abdomen where he would press a blade, were he in combat. He looked away. Below the rath, beyond the yellow furze, the red grove was cut and limbs lay askew, the foliage dead and gray. 'Dreams are the heart's vision,' he said quietly. 'They will only stop when the heart stops. When wolves cry outside the thorn hedges at Brí Léith, the women who have conceived have bad dreams. It's for the wolves' cry that the hawthorn is named. If they are cut in spring wolves come into the byre and kill the new calves.'

'She'll sleep better with a child beside her.'

'Then she is with child,' said Midhir, bowing his head. 'The kingship of Tara is blessed.'

'She is not, although her mare is already heavy with foal.'

Midhir unstrapped his shield, and turned it over. 'If you will play fidchell, I have a board and men that won't shame you.' The back of it was divided into squares of polished and blackened silver.

'Bring a table and benches from the hall,' Eochaidh called to his guards. 'We'll play fidchell under the sky. Many times I've played it all night before battle. A warrior's mind is sharp with death before him at first light, and the dead rising from their burned crannogs and byres to the stars. I've never lost a battle that followed fidchell.'

The guards put a table and two benches down in the grass. Midhir set the shield upon the table, then opened the bronze mail sack that was tied to his belt, and laid the fidchell pieces out on the shield. He gave the two oak-men to Eochaidh, one of yellow gold, a broad trunk flowing upwards into branches with leaves of thinnest gold foil; the other identical, but of pale rose gold. Each had a crack in the trunk filled with jet, the scorch mark of lightning.

'A fine set,' commented Eochaidh, grimly. He wanted silence now, Midhir saw, having said too much to a stranger; and although he was eager for the game, he would have liked more to fight Midhir hand to hand. 'If I'd known the bogs had such treasure, I would visit them more often. My chariots don't love that land; heavy wheels or light, they crawl, sink and splinter,' he said in a loud voice to the guards. He stood up and walked to the edge of the rath, looking down over the forest. The sun was just clearing the trees. 'Well, Midhir, I don't play without a stake.'

'Nor I. Name it, then.'

'It doesn't matter to me,' said Eochaidh, spreading his arms out to include all of Tara, and the land beyond. 'What I have desired I own. I don't know what you can afford to lose.'

Midhir said, 'I'll give you fifty dark grey horses with dappled blood-red heads, broad chests, slender limbs, huge, swift, but steady and easy to catch and guide with their enamelled reins. They will be in your fields at first light if I lose.'

Eochaidh stared at him. 'There are no such horses in Ireland,' he said. 'If you win I will give you fifty horses from my stables, the best in Ireland, with gilded bridles.'

'Agreed. Do you march your men straight across the board? And capture by enclosure?'

'Of course.'

'The one who attacks first always wins, if he has any skill at all. Have you the skill to play by the rule of hand?'

'No one plays that,' said Eochaidh.

'Of course it's much more difficult,' said Midhir, lightly.

'It might amuse me to learn this different play; the game grows stale.'

Midhir put his fists on his knees. 'As a child you played a game, "one, two, three" and your hands made the signs of axe, fire, blood. Fire burns axe, blood quenches fire, axe cuts to bring blood. In fidchell they are trees and shrubs that do battle; some as weapons that are made from their wood. Birch is axe: one finger, fire is furze: two fingers, alder bleeds: three fingers.

'One for birch, the axe wielder,
First tree in a barren land,
Cradle of forest,
First to lay a forest bare.

Two for rowan, the queen,
Who tames the mad horse with her stick,
Arms around the mad king, she sends lightning away.
Her funeral pyre brings the spirit army.

Three for alder, the piper,
Flood-bringer, he bleeds like a man.
Four for willow, moon.
Wicker and wave, she eases pain.

Five for ash, the king's throne,
Horseman, and strangler.
All for the queen's company, the right hand.

Pine follows next, archer,
First sigh and last, no remorse.
Furze is two, fire and thorn.
Heather is three, mead's flowers.

Aspen is four, silver and gold,
The heart's chatter.
Yew is five, the longbow.
Poisoner, he comes back.

Now for the king's company:
One for hawthorn, the wolf,
Raider of children and cattle.
Two for oak, the king, protector
Bringer of lightning.

Three for holly, the chariot.
Four for hazel, salmon of wisdom,
Imbas forosnai, foresight.

Five for the apple tree; she asks,
Who is my enemy?
Star hidden among flesh,
Fear closes the left hand in darkness.

Vine follows, who shall starve?
Ivy is two, the swan, traveller,
Broom, three, the fire
Blackthorn, the stick, skull smasher.
Elder, five, witch-horse
And corpse feeder.'

Midhir laid the fingers of his left hand across his right
forefinger; one finger, then two, making the signs of each
tree or shrub. 'On the right hand one is birch, two is rowan,
three is alder, four is willow, five is ash.' He switched
hands. 'On the left hand: hawthorn, oak, holly, hazel and

apple. Straight across the wrist are pine, furze, heather, aspen and yew; slanted across the wrist are vine, ivy, broom, blackthorn and elder.'

Eochaidh said, 'I've seen druids use these signs to share their secrets.'

'At one time the game was played with the hands; but now these signs remain only in the arrangement of the board.' Midhir set the pieces down, one in each square, black or silver, in two rows facing each other from far ends of the board. 'The trees of the right hand stand to the right in the first row, and those of the left stand to the left.'

'How do the pieces move, then?'

'Trees move diagonally, and shrubs forward and back. The lesser trees and shrubs move only one space. Oak and rowan move with the power of lightning,' said Midhir. Eochaidh turned the rowan with its copper berries in his hand. 'They may strike from any direction, to any distance.

'The fire shrubs — furze and broom — may burn continually in a row, taking men as they burn, until they reach an empty space. Willow and alder move diagonally, in the flood, taking anything in their path. Flood stops fire. The greater shrubs hawthorn, the wolf, and holly, the chariot, move any distance, and so may yew and ash,' said Midhir. 'If you take apple or yew you may retrieve a captured piece. And last of all, if rowan is taken, oak's power is diminished. He will have only the power of a plain tree or shrub to move one space, unless you can retrieve her; then he moves freely again. When the oak is taken, the game is won.'

'The forest is not safe for any man,' said Eochaidh, his hands trembling as he straightened his pieces on the board. 'Until all the woods are cut and the land is brought down to pasture under cattle, no man or woman is safe.'

'When that day comes fidchell will not be played; it will disappear out of the world, with bear and wolves and the old trees,' said Midhir. 'Before that day I would find my death.'

'On that day I will see my enemy from far off,' said Eochaidh, 'across the pasture and plains, and I'll be armed. No forging of weapons, no conspiracy will be hidden from me. My chariots will go wherever I send them. I will purify the land.'

'Nothing will live on it.'

'I will live on it, and my children will hold it after me.'

Midhir stood, his voice grown deep and loud. 'Then your children will despair, and not be grateful. The stars will not hold you if you destroy the land, and you will be dust under the wheels of your chariots.' Midhir saw Eochaidh's guards gather on the rath above them.

Eochaidh waved them back. 'It's good to play with an enemy whose weapons are unknown to me. But you too must judge me carefully, Midhir.' He laughed at his own joke, knowing that Midhir's name meant 'to judge'.

'I have not always been wise,' said Midhir, sitting down again.

'I see no wounds on you but the hawk's talons. You were lucky not to lose your eye.'

'It was no bird scarred me, but a sprig of holly.'

'From what tribe was this hollyman?'

'From Cleitech, on the bend of the Boyne, across the field from the Brugh of Aonghus.'

'No one lives there. No cattle graze there; it's poison land.'

'Then I'm mistaken.' Midhir held his fists out for Eochaidh to choose a king. Eochaidh touched the back of

Midhir's right hand, and took the rosegold king from his open palm.

Midhir said, 'Birch moves first: cradle wood, first tree to live on barren land. Weapon trees may leap over their own men as the game begins, just as arrows fly from bows in battle. Will you begin?'

Eochaidh moved his birch diagonally from the silver square in his rear line into the field, and Midhir followed with his own birch. They played slowly, moving minor pieces out, exchanging them. Eochaidh made no errors. Then Midhir brought his oak into the field.

Eochaidh sat back on his bench with his fingers lightly touching the edge of the board. He took Midhir's oak with his holly-chariot. 'That was a very stupid move. We had hardly begun. Too brief, too sad.'

Midhir stood up and swept the pieces into the sack. 'Tomorrow, then,' he said, 'you'll have the horses.'

'The day is just beginning. Let me show you Tara, and then we'll play again. You must see Étaín. All women are hags beside Étaín.'

'Keep the west gate open and you'll find the horses in your pasture tomorrow,' said Midhir, tying the sack to his belt. 'Give Étaín my good wishes for her rest. Tomorrow at noon, we'll play.' He bowed, turned and walked away, his spear slanting from his hand. Eochaidh watched him go out from the gate below and disappear into the woods.

Étaín was awake when Eochaidh came to her. He pulled her to him, looking at her face, saying, 'You lose your beauty, Étaín. You look like a slave, with that dark under your eyes.' She got up from the bed, putting a cloak around her, and laid turf on the fire.

'There was a man in Tara this morning who sends you his greeting. His name is Midhir, from Brí Léith.'

'And what brings Midhir of Brí Léith to Tara?' she asked quietly, facing the hearth.

'You know him then?'

'What is he like?'

'Very fair; like you, Étaín. He has a bad scar around one eye. Except for that you might call him beautiful.'

Étaín touched her eyelid lightly.

'He came to Tara to play fidchell with me,' he said.

'And did you play, Eochaidh?'

'Yes, and beat him too easily, by his own rules. He made a mistake that no fool would make.'

'You have no masters at fidchell.'

'I have no game to match his. A great treasure it is; I could hardly follow the game for looking at the pieces.'

'He's gone now, from Tara?'

'He is gone, and if there are not fifty grey horses with gold bridles in the field tomorrow we'll have a hunting party and bring his head for your threshold. Is he that rich a man or is he mad?'

'I don't know him, Eochaidh.'

'I can't understand how he got into Tara without anyone seeing him.'

'The hawk keeps the meadow quiet while she watches,' said Étaín.

'Hunger has marked him clearly. He wants to beat me.'

'They leave tracks behind them everywhere, the dead,' said Étaín. 'I've seen them in the forest.'

'What are you saying?'

'In my dreams they are alive. And always they play fidchell. "Who tames the mad horse with her rowan stick?" She's cruel. "Four for willow: moon, wicker and wave, she eases pain." The wind punishes. There's no place to rest. "The oak king comes, bringer of lightning." She clutched his arm. 'He's dangerous. Leave him alone, Eochaidh; he will destroy himself.'

'Stop your raving and come to me. Your eyes are ugly, but your skin is like silk.' He pulled her down on the bed, and moved her hair away from her neck, and kissed her.

The next morning Eochaidh walked down through the clearing of strewn red bark and rotting stumps to his west fields. The sun was just coming up, and beyond the banks of fire-furze a herd of dark grey horses grazed. Eochaidh went through a break in the hedge; wrens and sparrows fluttered out, their wings nearly touching him. The horses were big chested, wide girthed with good bone and delicate heads, haltered in gold, their grey coats going red at the eyes and ears, the way bare hills turn crimson at sunset. Their tails were long and thick, blood red as their manes.

Midhir found him walking in the rain along the rath.

'I've sent the hostages out of the hall, and had the table brought inside,' said Eochaidh, walking beside him up the hill. His guards saluted as they went past. 'Name the stake.'

'You shall have from me fifty young boars, curly, mottled, grey-bellied, blue-backed, with horses' hooves on them, and a vat of blackthorn to cook them in.

'And the next day fifty gold-hilted swords, and after that fifty red-eared cows with white red-eared calves and a bronze spancel on each calf. And then fifty grey wethers with red heads, three-horned. Then fifty ivory-hilted swords. Then fifty royal speckled cloaks.'

'Play well, Eochaidh, before this boasting dies,' said Fedach, as they entered the hall.

'He trades his life for the stake, if he loses and doesn't pay. Come Midhir, let's play fidchell.' Eochaidh took the silver shield and laid it carefully on the table beside the fire, then arranged the gold trees and shrubs upon it. The day passed and the hall grew dark, and they had played one hundred moves before a piece was lost. There were no lightning advances and retreats by the oak; no retaliations by the rowan. All the pieces of greatest power were quiet.

When Eochaidh called for torches, they exchanged rowans. Midhir surrounded his oak with hazel, apple, elder and vine, but Eochaidh had still the wolf-hawthorn, that could move as many spaces as he wished, and he approached the oak in siege. There was an open space next to Midhir's vine, and Eochaidh moved his hawthorn there. Midhir took it with his vine. But Eochaidh's willow was aligned with vine and oak, and in one move he flooded through them both, and the game was his.

The next day there were giant blue-backed boars in the oak woods. The royal huntsman brought back huge hooves and tusks for proof, and the scent of roast boar went through the hall where Midhir and Eochaidh played. Summer passed, and still Eochaidh won, and every morning afterwards he found what Midhir had promised.

One night Fedach came to Eochaidh as he polished the blades of the fifty ivory-hilted swords, for it was Eochaidh's custom to let no one touch his weapons. The druid asked, 'Where does Midhir get his wealth?'

'That would make a good story,' Eochaidh answered. 'See how smooth and yellow the ivory is, Fedach. Like tallow they are; warm as softened wax in your hand. Like holding a man's hand, to hold this weapon and run him through.'

Fedach said, 'A good story; that's what you would get. Who is he? Who are his kin? Why does he come here to lose his treasure? I'm afraid for you, for all of us. I can't see his plan.'

'He comes to play fidchell, that's all. If he has dug up the graves of his kin to get treasure, it's not my concern. Don't watch me, as if I were a child. It would please me more if you watched Étaín; she has the look of death on her now.'

'Not the poorest farmer in Tara would keep a beast with red ears,' said Fedach. 'They bring bad luck.'

'They're an ancient breed, flesh and blood, like Midhir himself. We have played fidchell. I know him well; I know how he wages war.'

'When he asks what stake you will play for, demand an impossible thing. He'll bargain with you, then. Don't you want to see what he keeps back?'

'Will you be satisfied then? Be calm, Fedach. I welcome the challenge. When he has no treasure left I'll kill him. Fidchell is a distraction; any man can be killed while he plays the game.'

'That is forbidden.'

'That's your business.' Then he sent Fedach away.

But the next day when Midhir came to the gate of Tara, driving a cart filled with royal cloaks, each woven with nine colors, the guards stopped him.

Midhir got down from the cart, and took his sword from his belt. The guards raised their spears against him. 'No one passes today without the king's permission,' said the captain.

'I play fidchell with the king,' said Midhir.

'No man,' repeated the captain. Then Midhir saw Eochaidh riding along the rath, and the king saw him, and turned his horse, coming down to the gate. He dismounted and walked past Midhir to the cart, putting his hands through the cloaks, inspecting them. He nodded and came to Midhir.

'Here is the stake I will play for, and no other. If I win today make a road for me to travel swiftly to Brí Léith,' said Eochaidh, grinning. 'You will pull down my forest to the west and build me a road over the bogs so that my chariots may run fast to my stronghold Dun Fremain, and to Connaught where my enemies lie, and to the fields of Brí Léith, where the red-eared cattle graze.'

Midhir was silent. Rage filled him, and the desire was great in him to kill Eochaidh where he stood. But he said lightly, 'You lay too much on me.'

'Not at all.'

'I wouldn't do this if I had the power,' said Midhir.

'Then I regret this weakness in you,' said Eochaidh. 'And you are no opponent for me.' As he turned away Midhir grabbed his arm. The guards pressed their spears against him. Eochaidh stared at Midhir, then nodded to his guards, and they stepped back. Midhir released him. 'If I win today you will clear the woods and build my road, and I'll be satisfied. Perhaps I shall lose. But that is the stake or I won't play fidchell with you.'

'Then let no man or woman go out of doors until sunrise tomorrow,' said Midhir, his voice low.

'If I say it, it shall be done. Now come into Tara, and we'll play.'

That day Midhir lost again. When he was gone Eochaidh gave orders to his guards that all men and women should immediately drive their animals inside, and stay themselves within their walls until sunrise. But he sent Ailill secretly into the bog.

Ailill watched the west from his hiding place in a copse of blackthorn. At dusk men began to gather, more men than he had ever seen. They came out of the west with carts and oxen, and they came like starlings before winter that fill the sky, passing for hours overhead. They stripped off their clothes for battle, making a hill of their cloaks for Midhir to stand upon and give his orders. But they had no weapons on them, and they didn't fight but went to work digging a long trench. They worked without resting, their bodies wet and shining as the moon came up. Soon the deep furrow disappeared over the distant rise. Then the oxen, yoked about the shoulders, as no man of Ireland had ever before harnessed them, were driven to the trench with carts of stones and rushes, and some dragging oak trees. The men heaved stones into the trench, and laid the rushes in after. Ailill heard them sing,

'Put here, put there
Good oxen;
In the hours after sundown the work is hard,
And all the beasts suffer.
No one knows whose is the gain,
Whose is the loss
From the causeway over the bog of Meath.'

They laid the oaks side by side to make a road above the soft wet ground. By daybreak the men and oxen were gone. There was no movement on the bog, except two crows who flew down to inspect the road.

Ailill went to the hall and told Eochaidh what he had seen. Eochaidh went out of the fort, his guards and Fedach following, and as they came down the hill they saw that Ailill had not lied.

But as they reached the new road, they saw Midhir himself come riding in a hard gallop towards them, his horse's head pulled down to the side to keep him from bolting. Midhir held him to the road, with his spear out straight, and no clothing on him but his weapon belt. He came fast, and veered away just before he reached them. He turned his maddened horse in a tight circle, the animal covered with foam and terrified by the feel of the road, by the sound of his hooves striking the timber.

'Stand back, Eochaidh of Tara. You have laid great hardship on me, and then betrayed me,' cried Midhir, turning the horse, his long spear dividing the air.

'The road pleases me,' said Eochaidh.

'You sent spies into the bog after me, and broke our trust. And because you didn't trust me, because you sent a spy to watch me, it's not perfect. But nothing will be changed, nothing added or taken away.'

'I accept it,' said Eochaidh. 'You have fulfilled the bargain.'

Midhir turned his horse close to him. 'I would have made something else to please you. But now my mind is set against you.' Eochaidh and his men stood back, silent. Midhir felt the sun warm on the sweat of his back. Steam rose up from his horse's neck. A hawk flew over them. 'Now shall we play fidchell?' he asked quietly, lowering his spear.

'Choose the stake,' said Eochaidh. 'What shall it be?'

'The prize that either of us shall wish,' said Midhir. 'Do not name it.'

'Agreed,' said Eochaidh. 'Go on, then, we'll ride to Tara.'

'Not today. I'm tired of being watched.'

'Where will you play?'

'In the oak grove beyond the Queen's Bed. You and I will play alone.'

'Would it be wise to play with our backs to the forest? There are wolves—'

'Then bring a guard who has skill casting a spear, and let him watch for you, but keep him out of my sight.'

'I have no quarrel with that,' said Eochaidh, turning his horse, and they rode to the woods.

CHAPTER 2

The Forest

ÉTAÍN HEARD THE HORSES coming, breaking foliage in the woods. When she came out of the house she saw Midhir ride up beside Eochaidh.

Eochaidh dismounted and gave the reins to his guard. 'Here is Midhir of Brí Léith,' he said to Étaín, taking her by both arms. 'Greet him if he's no stranger to you.'

'You are welcome, Midhir.'

'I keep her close; she walks in her sleep,' said Eochaidh, standing behind her, lifting the hair from her shoulders, kissing her. 'Is she beautiful, Midhir?'

Midhir bowed his head slightly. 'Beautiful any until Étaín. You're well?'

She left Eochaidh and went to Midhir and gave him her hand. 'I am.' She lightly touched the scar beside his eye and then withdrew her hand. 'What stake do you play for today, Midhir?'

'Whoever wins names it,' he said. 'Étaín, will you give me a strand of your hair for my spear?'

She pulled out a long gold strand and laid it across his palm. He wound it underneath the five-starred spear head, and made a knot to finish it. He pulled an apple off the branch above him, and split it with the spear. The bronze barbs glistened. He gave her the fruit, saying softly, 'Who is my enemy? Where does he lie? How will I destroy him?'

She answered,

'My enemy is fear,
He lies in the heart.
His hunger is mine,
Our cause is just,
He is my ally,
My enemy destroyed.'

She turned around to face Eochaidh. 'I have seen a tame boar go mad and destroy the woods in his fury. I have seen a cold white mountain explode like a jar dropped on stone, and his blood scorch the air.' She turned back to Midhir. 'No dream, Midhir; I know you well enough. And I haven't been afraid of wolves since I heard them sing on the bogs near Dun Fremain.'

Eochaidh said, 'She speaks nonsense. The sun will go no higher today. I don't want to be in the woods at nightfall. Let's go.'

When Eochaidh followed Midhir into the forest, it was as if he walked from day into night, he could see no shred of sky through the canopy. Birds flew higher into the trees as he pushed branches away before him. Moss cloaked the tree trunks, his feet sank into thick moss and leaves; he waded through chest high ferns, like a hundred sword blades, their points unfurled. Leaves were still thick on the branches; it was impossible to see far into the woods.

They came out into a small clearing. Midhir pointed to the ground and the servants set down the table and the small benches. They looked around them, but didn't move.

'Go on! Leave us!' ordered Eochaidh. 'What, are you already lost?'

Midhir pointed back in the direction they had come. They disappeared quickly into the trees, and the guard followed them. After the leaves swallowed him, he made no noise. The forest was very still. Midhir sang softly as he laid the pieces out on his shield; Eochaidh watched the woods for movement.

'In the beginning of the world
There were pines on the mountains, and great deer;
Pines on Brí Léith, and a wolf;
Pines on Knowth, and an amber cat;
Pines on Slievenamon, and two swans.
Birch, rowan, alder, willow followed.
Oak in the valleys, wielding lightning;
Hazel stood guard over the well in the Boyne;
Ash made a throne at Uisnech;
Yew closed the gate at Cruachan.'

When he had finished arranging the board Midhir said, 'Your move,' and Eochaidh led out his birch. Midhir followed. Eochaidh moved his pine into the field, and Midhir moved his ash out; Eochaidh followed with ash.

Midhir looked off into the forest. Eochaidh followed his glance; but heard nothing. Still Midhir didn't touch the board. 'It's getting dark. And cold. You're wasting time,' said Eochaidh, his voice too loud. 'Make your move,' he said.

Midhir moved his apple out into the field. Eochaidh put his hand on his ash quickly, ready to take the apple, then hesitated. He considered how he might turn this chance into a more deadly move, one that would end the game quickly. It was getting so dark that it was difficult to see the shield well; there was little difference in the squares. It was as though he held his hand under a murky lake. And it was very quiet. He looked up. Midhir was gone.

Eochaidh stood, turning the bench over. He walked into the trees, and quickly found the place of crushed grass and briars where the guard had been, but there was no one. An ash bow, an arrow of holly, a bronze axe with a birch handle and a blackthorn stick were laid out upon the trampled grass. He took the weapons out into the clearing.

He listened for movement in the forest. There was a distant sound of water, and close by, at the edge of the birches, a faint rustling. The noise was too tentative and too varied for something that stalked or was being hunted. It was the sound of something that moved without fear, on its own business.

He went through the birches and into the pines. The rustling stopped the moment he entered them. As he went on the sound of water grew and now he heard the dim mutter of frogs. The pines gave way to alders as the ground fell and grew wetter. The frogs were quiet. There was movement in the reeds ahead that hid the stream, and then a sudden shrill piping. He saw a flash of white skin through the reeds. He knelt into his bow, strung it, put an arrow into the string, and aimed. He shot, and something fell, shaking the reeds. He hooked the bow over his shoulder, picked up the axe and stick and walked to the stream.

There was no sign of man or animal at the bank, only alder, ferns and cress. He pulled his arrow out of the trunk of an alder, and blood ran down the smooth grey bark, in a slow pulse.

'Someone has taken my kill. The pipe was a signal. Where are you, Midhir?' he said softly to himself. He ran his finger along the blade to feel its edge, and his finger was stained black. He touched his tongue; it tasted of salt.

He headed back into the pines, holding the axe and stick before him as two shields. The ground was rising and the pines went on but he saw no birches. He came to a hedge of hawthorn, growing thick and high with no way around or through it. He found a weak place in the wall and plunged in. Thorns caught his cloak, his hair. He struggled to pull free, cursing, but he was trapped. He swung his axe, the thorns biting his arms and face, but gradually a hole grew in the hedge, and he was through. He knelt, untangling his cloak, hair and skin from the thorns. It was very quiet. He thought of how much noise he had made. Like a hare caught in a briar, he had struggled, his heart racing, his skin sweating fear. And if there was a wolf, he would come.

Eochaidh looked up and saw the wolf staring at him. He was long-legged and silver-maned, with wide shoulders, and eyes the colour of corn. The wolf swayed, watching him. He growled softly.

'Cut the hawthorn, and I will come.
Where are your children? Your new born calves?
Give me your lambs, white as thorn blossoms,
Lord of Tara, king of oak,
Then I won't drink the blood of your throat.'

The wolf came up closer, standing over Eochaidh's blackthorn stick, his head lowered, watching him. Eochaidh kept very still.

Then the wolf turned and ambled off into the woods. Eochaidh lunged toward his axe, grabbed it, hurled it hard. The blade caught the wolf behind the ears, and he went straight down. Eochaidh wrenched himself free from the thorns and ran to the wolf. His back was broken. He smashed his skull with the blackthorn stick, then stepped over the body. He walked on through oak saplings, swinging his axe wide with each step, branches falling with each sweep of the axe. He thought only about weapons. Midhir had his bronze spear; it was not as powerful as iron but true enough to drop a man if the aim was right.

He came upon an oak with an enormous rough dappled silver trunk; scarlet mushrooms grew in the lee of its roots. Flames appeared and disappeared among the clustered leaves, among the branches in the huge crown. A purple butterfly floated down, settling on a lower branch. Two dark eyes watched him from the bottom of its wings.

There was a woman standing in front of the tree, a woman in a dress of green silk, with a purple fleece cape over her shoulders, and her yellow hair loose around her. Her feet were white on the leaves. She sank slowly to kneel in the leaves, and Eochaidh saw a young man lying before her, naked, his arms flung out, blood staining his face and his side. It was the guard, dead, with a spear in him. The woman leaned over him, and licked the blood from his face.

But when Eochaidh stepped closer he saw that it was only the purple butterfly perched lightly on a rotting young rabbit; the butterfly was eating its flesh.

Suddenly it flew off. There was a step behind him; something with too much weight to be silent.

Midhir stood watching him. The butterfly settled on his shoulder. The wolf came up behind him and lay down at his heels. He held his spear out straight; there was an apple on the point.

'Who are you?' cried Eochaidh. 'You have deceived me. What kind of man are you?'

Midhir said, 'I have loved her for a thousand years.'

Eochaidh shot a holly arrow into his eye, and he fell.

'Well, he can die,' said Eochaidh to the woods. He picked up Midhir's spear and walked past him, downhill through pines and gnarled, ancient yews, the scent of them sharp.

It wasn't long before he saw the white birches, and then the clearing ahead, and the fidchell table. A man was sitting on a bench before the table with his back to him. It was Midhir's back, his gold hair. Was there someone else in the forest, who had placed Midhir's corpse there to taunt him? Eochaidh walked out into the clearing, the spear tight in his hand. Midhir turned around. 'Your move,' he said.

There was no mark on him, just the fine clean scars around his eye. Eochaidh sat down slowly.

'You're in danger,' said Midhir. 'My yew is now threatening your oak.'

'Yew?' He looked at the fidchell board.

'When an old yew dies, a new tree is born from the dead. One who plays fidchell to win must know the forest.'

'We have exchanged rowans?'

'Of course.' Midhir's voice became terrible. 'Do you accuse me of cheating?'

'I do not,' said Eochaidh, his hands trembling.

'"Be not uneasy, my friend." When I make the first cut on an old tree, before I put my mouth to the wound, drinking the sap, we are allies. "Be not uneasy, my friend."'

But you refuse to understand me. Your fear is great; you make an enemy strong.'

'I have no weapons left to defend him,' he mumbled, moving his birch in front of his oak.

Midhir moved his yew away from the oak.

Eochaidh moved the birch again, threatening the yew.

Midhir took his oak with his yew.

Eochaidh looked off into the woods. 'What is the stake that you choose?'

'My arms around Étaín and a kiss from her,' said Midhir, rising from the table.

Eochaidh stared at him, stunned.

'That is what I shall have,' said Midhir, louder. The guard came out of the forest; others followed, Ailill among them. 'To hold Étaín.'

'Go from me,' screamed Eochaidh. 'Come back in one month and you'll have it.'

Midhir went past Eochaidh's men into the woods.

Eochaidh walked out of the forest with Ailill beside him. The guards went before and behind, keeping their distance. 'He wants to be High King of Tara. That's what he wants. Why didn't I see it?'

'Why didn't you kill him?' whispered Ailill.

'Before the guards? They saw him win. I couldn't kill them all, and you, as well. I have a month; a month is enough time. I'll call warriors from Dun Fremain, from every tuath in Ireland. He won't get close to Tara. I won't be fooled again by his tricks. He wants to be High King. Well, he's more fool than I thought. He'll be dead when he steps on the first stone of the royal road, the road he made, where my chariots will run, and his blood.'

CHAPTER 3

Defence of Tara

FROM THE RAMPARTS of Tara Étaín watched Eochaidh's army gather. His messengers had gone out on Midhir's grey horses, each bearing a treasure of Brí Léith to be carefully unwrapped before a hearth fire, showing a glimpse of gold or bronze. And for such treasures, for the promise of stallions, or a fine red bull, the chieftains and warriors of Ireland came to Tara to make the fort strong against Eochaidh's enemy. They came on horseback and on foot, with chariots and rattling carts filled with harness and weapons.

As far as Étaín could see, from the high, inner wall where she was allowed to walk, there wasn't a tree standing that would give shade to a colt or calf in summer. The woods around Tara had been clear cut for weapons, and chariots. Alders were stripped from creekbanks for charcoal for the forging; slow burning oak and ash to keep the forge fires hot. Birch fell for axe handles and arrowshafts, with scraps saved for kindling. Yews were cut for bows; yew berries pressed for poison for the arrow tips. They took willow for chariot spokes, ash for rims and elm for the hubs. The smith fires were never cold, and the sky was black with campfires and smithfires, many more than had been kindled at the feis one year past.

There were weapons forged even on the Mound of the Hostages. Although Samhain approached, the lengthening nights were counted off instead towards Midhir's return, with little regard for druids' rites. Étaín was not allowed outside the ramparts of the fort, but she walked often along the wall, even in rain; and Eochaidh said that it was good that she did not hide her beauty from his army, that she would make them brave when war came.

After the forests were cut deer were plentiful, and there were boar and wolves sighted in the fields, but soon these disappeared. As days passed more men came into Tara, and food grew scarce. The oak and hazel were felled before the nuts were fully ripened, and the pigs were eaten, for there was no mast to keep them. Cattle and sheep were taken from the farmers to feed the army, and if a family had only a single cow remaining to them they had to bleed her to feed themselves. Étaín saw her own white mare harnessed to a chariot; there were no horses in Tara that did not belong to Eochaidh's army.

Farmers began to shout at Étaín when they saw her. She would nod grimly at any words from below, curse or praise. One day an old woman threw a stick at her, calling her caillech, hag, and then Eochaidh said he wouldn't risk the people's anger by taking their weapons away, so he forbade Étaín to leave the hall until dusk, when she might walk between four guards, with her head covered.

It was rumoured among the people that the enemy had weapons of magical power and this was confirmed by the druid Fedach, who said that Midhir was not a man. He said that the army of Tara would be victorious by the power of the iron weapons they carried, but that the enemy was not to be bargained with, being a remnant of something past, like a beast or spirit that lingered in an ancient forest or cairn. And such a cairn was home to Midhir, and his weapons were famine and plague, and these he could bring into Tara on Samhain, the night when the dead cross over. But it was hunger that drove out fear and fuelled anger against rich Midhir, and the warriors grew afraid that Midhir would not come.

Near Samhain the wind blew from the east, and there was frost on the self-heal. The seabirds' dark faces turned white, and barnacle geese were seen on the shore. Cows cried in the dark to be milked, calling the people early from their beds; and they cursed them, for they woke hungry, and it was only sleep that could dull their hunger. As the days grew shorter Eochaidh told them that if they died before Tara's walls, their kin would live like kings on Midhir's gold.

Samhain came, and Eochaidh's army camped below the ramparts, and deep along the road to Brí Léith. There were fires in the bogs; the hill of Tara was ablaze with light. Eochaidh kept Étaín beside him in the hall, sending instructions by messengers to his captains all day. Ailill came in at dusk from the western road to report that no army gathered there.

Étaín sat staring into the fire, a wolfhound quiet at her feet. Smoke hung under the rafters. The room grew dim and cold, and the sky black in the smokehole. Through the open door of the hall she heard horses neighing, pipes and the bodhran. She pulled a blanket over her white robe; Eochaidh had ordered her to wear her wedding clothes for Samhain, and to paint gold spirals on her temples and shoulders. A servant stopped before her with a plate of food. She took a piece of meat for the dog only; the smell of it sickened her.

On the other side of the firepit a man sat with his back to her, his head lowered. He wore a heavy drab cloak, but no chains bound him to the bench, so she thought that he was not a hostage. If he were a warrior, perhaps it was the sadness that he might be lost to his family that made him so pensive. Then he stood, and Eochaidh turned, and Étaín saw a look of terror come on Eochaidh's face. Ailill and the other men backed away.

Midhir unpinned the cloak and showed himself to Eochaidh, a gold torc around his neck, a bronze sword in his hand.

Eochaidh said quickly, 'You see I expected you tonight, but you startled me. You've come alone. Where's your army? I didn't expect lunacy from one who plays fidchell so well when it suits him. You see that I have you surrounded, and you have no allies in Tara. Your end will be quick; there are no moves remaining.' His men drew their swords and stepped forward.

'I've come to claim what I won at fidchell,' said Midhir.

'Your arms around Étaín and a kiss from her,' laughed Eochaidh. 'Your death, you mean.'

'Yours, I think,' said Midhir. 'Your doom will come when you give Étaín away. That is your geis.'

'Who told you those words?' cried Eochaidh, his voice shaking with anger. 'You want Tara, Midhir? You shall have it; your head upon my gate this winter, where Étaín shall watch it slowly rot.'

'Perhaps,' he said quietly, turning to Étaín. 'You promised to come with me if your husband would give you away.'

'I keep my bargains,' said Eochaidh. 'Go on. Put your arms around her. Touch her skin, her breasts; take her before us all, and then I kill you.'

Midhir spoke in a low voice to Étaín,

'Come with me now, Bé Find,
To Slievenamon, hill of the moon,
That land where peace is.
There is neither mine nor thine,
No hunger, no sickness,
There death cannot come.

Oh woman of Light, Bé Find,
If you come with me,
To my people,
A crown of gold shall be on your head,
Honey, ale, fresh milk
You will have with me.

Come to my bed of soft lake rushes,
Our bed high upon the mountain,
There no one follows,
But the wind, our bodhran.
There in the mist we are safe,
Bé Find, now come with me.'

She answered him,

'This place shall be a land of desolation;
War comes to us and to Eochaidh,
Battle against many thousands
And the Brugh shall be destroyed.

None that watch the stars from the hilltops
Will know that you and I rest there,
In the dark where night is made,
The wind our breath soft
Upon the spreading lake.

Oh, you will not die alone,
Midhir of Brí Léith,
While I love you.'

She walked to him and put her arms around his neck and kissed him. He brought his sword across her back, his other arm around her waist, bringing her close.

For a moment the room was still.

Then someone screamed, and it seemed that Étaín's cloak had caught fire, and flames were rushing up over them both, standing close together, their lips pressed together, their eyes closed. And the flames went high, to the rafters, and Midhir held Étaín as they rose up through the chimneyhole and they were gone from the hall.

Where they had stood pieces of ash floated in the air. Eochaidh and his guards ran outside. There a crowd had gathered. They yelled, pointing at the sky, at two swans flying over Tara. The moon was coming up in the southern sky, and they watched the swans cross the moon, and disappear.

'He's stolen her!' screamed Eochaidh. 'I'll dig up every mound in Ireland until I find the woman. There will be gold for everyone—do you hear me—I swear it! We go south to the mountain tonight. Get my horses ready!' And from the rampart, and the hillside, and the fields below, the army answered him with one voice, 'Eochaidh King!'

CHAPTER 4

Slievenamon —Hill of the Moon

THAT NIGHT THE ROAD south was alive with men and horses. Torches moved down into the dense oak forests. Eochaidh's men rode fast, and when the sun came up they saw the heights of Slievenamon, violet, blurred by mist, in the distance.

That night Midhir and Étaín slept on Slievenamon, and when they woke before dawn, they held each other and watched swans pass over the mountain.

'Look at this stone I found beside me,' said Midhir, giving it to Étaín.

It fit into her palm. 'How beautiful it is,' she said, 'like a jewel.' She turned it over in the moonlight. 'But the colour is blood, and the shape is the heart of an animal.'

Midhir closed his hand over hers.

'Eochaidh will come,' said Étaín.

'You came willingly,' he said, kissing her hand. 'The rest is the fight of every Samhain season. Two stags in one meadow; crowns locked together.'

'In no season does war come to beasts,' she said. 'Only we make enemies of strangers.'

'Holding land for our own, as though we could live forever,' said Midhir.

'Tonight at least there will be no blood shed.'

Étaín lay back against him, and they were silent.

'The wind is soft,' she whispered, 'and you are beside me. I cannot imagine war.'

His arms encircled her; he felt the faint pulse in her temple against his cheek.

'Do you remember me, Étaín?' he asked, quietly.

After a moment she said, 'Will you ask me that now? Will you be sad if I cannot answer? Midhir, I would not say so, being sure, though the feel of your body on mine wakes me; your skin warm against mine, a kindling I have known before. But is the shape of your shoulder that I seem to know the shape of each man's body that I have touched? And these stones, this heather, grey with wind, have I not known them always?

'And if I do not remember you, Midhir, or if I love the shape of this wave coming toward me, for its own sake, or because I loved the one that came before, how can I be certain? Does it matter, then? I think I have loved you before, for the ache in me now is great; but so it comes to me standing beneath the stars, lonely for the sea and the shape of a mountain I have never seen, except in a dream.'

'No matter, Étaín.' Midhir covered her with his cloak. 'Sleep now, and I'll tell you about Aonghus, who was dear to me, and your friend.'

'Tell me, Midhir, about Aonghus.'

'I will,' he whispered, 'for he's not lost to us.'

'Aonghus sleeps in the Brugh and dreams.

A woman comes to him, stands below his bed;

A cloak of swans down over her white skin,
Her hair, the colour of yew berries, bound with silver.
She plays the bodhran.
Like the slow heartbeat of a bear sleeping his winter
sleep,
Like a cat moving slowly along the roof of a house,
She summons dusk, night, the stars and first light,
Calls winter and summer out of the east.
She looks at him long;
He wakes; she is gone.

'That day he walks his land
With the dream blurred but heavy on him.
Night comes, he lies on his bed,
And remembers:
Black eyes and red hair.
She comes;
That night and the night after,
Stands in his dream, drumming;
Waking, he neither eats nor speaks,
With the weight of longing for her.

'The year comes round again;
Aonghus sick and healers called to him.
Fergne comes, who knows by smoke
From a house, by a man's face,
What illness holds him.
"It's love in absence that weakens you.
Separated from your love,
Sick at heart, you tell no one."
Aonghus answers, "You've seen my heart."

'Fergne sends for his mother Bóinn.

Elcmhar dead, she comes from Cleitech,
Wading the ford of the Boyne
To his bed in the Brugh.
He tells the likeness of the woman;
Bóinn swears to find her, but a year passes,
And Aonghus still fails.

'Then Bóinn seeks the Daghdha,
No longer lord of Uisnech,
He grows strange, avoids men.
But Aonghus will die;
So all travellers speak the Daghdha's name
Until word comes from the woods
Below the Boyne
That he is found.

'Bóinn tracks him in the forest.
She comes close, hears him breathe in the trees,
The shape of his shoulder only through the branches
above her.
Fierce and shy as a wild boar, he hides.
Bóinn speaks gently, but
Aonghus will die.
The Daghda answers, hoarse and halting,
"Go to Bodb; he's king of the sidhe."
A crash of branches and he is gone.

'Bodb rules Slievenamon.
From this mountain his men search
For the shape of her child's dream;
One year gone and they return,
The woman found close by,
At the Lake of the Dragon's Mouth.

'At the Brugh chariots are harnessed
And Aonghus driven by the river road,
West to Tara, south to Slievenamon.
Beside the Lake of the Dragon
Aonghus hides, watching.
One hundred women swim in the lake,
Each pair bound by a silver chain,
But one by gold, of greater height and beauty;
He knows her.

'Caer Ibormeith she is, the cluster of yew berries,
Daughter of Ethal from Sidhe Uamuin in Connaught.
Then the Daghdha goes to Ailill, king of Connaught.
Together they destroy the sidhe of Ethal Anbuail,
Taking many heads of his kin.
But Ethal cannot give his daughter away;
She can be taken on Samhain only,
At the Lake of the Dragon's Mouth.

'At Samhain Aonghus and the Daghdha watch,
Beside the deep lake where a hundred swans drift,
Each pair bound by silver chains,
But one in gold.
Mist pours up, winter's breath,
The dragon sleeps.
Aonghus dreams; if he moves,
Frightened, she'll leave him.
"Call her to you," the Daghdha tells him.
And goes into the forest, then.
He will not be found again.

'Aonghus kneels at the lake.

He calls, his voice low, a flute;
Sad as the wolf's cry,
But no blood in it,
Of wind running along ice.

"Come and talk with me, Caer!"
She turns but keeps back from the shore.
"Who calls me?" she asks.
"It is Aonghus."
"I will come," she says, "But swear
That I'll return."
He swears and she comes close.
He walks into the water until he reaches her,
His arms around her, stroking her wings,
He becomes her shape.

'Three times they drift around the lake,
Drowsy with sleep,
Then rise up together,
Wings moving together,
To the bodhran,
The sky between them locked
By a chain of air.
Down they come to the mound of the Brugh;
There sing, and peace comes on
The cattle and the men of the land.

'Time comes when cattle graze on the mound of the
Brugh,
The stones dissolve in a thousand years of rain,
Aonghus is gone from the Brugh.
Now he lives alone in the west;
In the fort of his name

From the cliff edge where he dreams,
He strikes the bodhran of the deep sea
And sends living waves to Ireland.'

'Now rest,' said Midhir, holding Étaín in his arms. 'No
bad dreams come to the height of Slievenamon.'

'Sleep, Étaín,
Fold your dreams now
Under your wings,
Silken, white.
The lake is still,
Drift and sleep.'

Eochaidh's army reached the foot of Slievenamon. They
followed the cattle track up the east side of the mountain,
and stopped halfway at dusk, in the fields around a small
house. When the herdsman brought his cows down from
the mountain, Eochaidh's men killed them and feasted.

'How do we find the cairn on Slievenamon?' asked
Eochaidh of the herdsman and his wife. They told him they
had never seen a cairn, but there was only one path up to
the top, the old track they drove their sheep and cattle along
to graze on the heather when the grass was spare.

'You're lying,' said Eochaidh. 'What does Midhir pay
you to hide him? You're his slaves, don't deny it.'

'We know no one of that name,' said the woman, kneeling before him. 'No one lives on the mountain above this
place,' she said, twisting the edge of his cloak.

Eochaidh knocked the woman aside. 'It's not Midhir that
can defend you, is it? Now,' said Eochaidh, turning to the
man, 'what will you tell me about the mound on Slievenamon?'

'Maybe I have seen it. The mist comes in fast on Slievenamon. Maybe there is something up there.'

'Something. What?'

'Stones. And light, that comes and goes on the mountain.'

'Campfires. Tell me now about weapons. How many men are camped there? Do they have horses? Are there trees beyond that ridge, around the cairns? Where can men hide?'

'No men on the mountain, no weapons. Horses maybe, and swans, but no men.'

'Tomorrow you'll lead us to the cairn and the swans' nest.'

The next morning they started up the mountain, following the narrow shepherd's track along a stream bed, where there was only a trickle of water running now. They reached the mist. The woods were shallow with fog; the trees black-trunked close by, grey at a spear's cast, wraith-white shapes beyond. Then they came out of the fog, and the sun rose, filling the mist and the crowns of the trees with gold, lining each trunk with gold.

They climbed higher and the trees gave way to hawthorn and furze and rough brown heather, and the wind made it hard to walk. Then the path narrowed and disappeared. Above them rose a mound the width of six oxen, standing head to tail. The cairn faced east with three stones making a threshold. Eochaidh walked up to a fire pit and stirred the ash with his sword. 'Build a fire, here,' he said to his men, and then he turned, facing the threshold. He held his shield at an angle which caught the sun's glare and reflected it into the cairn. The light from his shield moved over the stones inside the passageway, showing carvings of spirals and crescents, and waving lines, but no sign of man or woman.

'See here, the signs of sorcery,' he said, showing Ailill and his captains. 'You've seen them before. The same as in the foul cave in the Brugh.'

'If there is anyone on this mountain, surely they know we're here,' said Ailill.

'Here is the hiding place of evil,' said Eochaidh. 'Tell the men not to be afraid; they must take the cairn apart. Fedach will make a purifying sacrifice. And tell the men that any gold or treasure they find inside belongs to them.'

That day and for many days after, with ropes and axes and spades Eochaidh's men dug out the threshold stones of the cairn, and laid them bare, but there was no gold to be found under them. The first night on the top of Slievenamon the mist came in, and then a flood of bats came from the mouth of the cairn. The men screamed and swung their swords in the fog, and ran in their terror, falling, and some were cut by their own weapons. But except for the bats, nothing moved inside the cave; Eochaidh set a watch by day and night. He sent men out to search for nests, with orders to spear any swans that they found, for they were the disguise of sorcerers, he said, and while there were swans in Ireland no decent person was safe, for who could tell beyond the shape of a creature what it might be? But they found no swans on the mountain.

After a week passed and no gold had been found, Eochaidh's captain came to Ailill and told him that the men wouldn't follow Eochaidh much longer.

'It's slow work moving the stones,' said Ailill. 'But there's gold. You yourself heard Midhir promise it to Étaín.'

'I heard him. But what did you see?'

'What everyone saw. Two swans circling the hill. Flying off south.'

'No, before that. Inside. In the hall.'

'It was dark. I'm not sure. But maybe I saw two people burn to death,' Ailill said softly.

'And the king put his torch to their cloaks.'

'A man has stolen a woman before.'

'There were fifty of us surrounding him in the hall that night.'

'And how did he get into Tara?' asked Ailill.

'The king let him in. He wanted war.'

'He's coming, now, be quiet.'

'Come with me quickly, and bring your swords,' said Eochaidh. 'There's someone up there.'

They followed him to the cairn. A woman stood among the stones that Eochaidh's men had pulled from the entrance. She was trying to turn a stone over.

'You moved the stones,' she said. 'The moon is coming in. How will she find her way?'

'You're trespassing here. It's Eochaidh, High King, who stands before you now. Do you know Midhir? Do you know where he is?'

'Why are you destroying Slievenamon? There is no one here you seek. Midhir is king of the sidhe, his fortress is Brí Léith. Go to Brí Léith, and leave us in peace.'

'To Brí Léith? Yes, he would run for the protection of his fort, of his warriors. If you have lied it will be an easy thing to come back here and finish what we began. Sorcerors are not welcome in Ireland anymore.'

'We have not interfered with you. Leave us in peace.'

'Every hill has an unclean place on it. A man can't look on the horizon without seeing the shape of a mound.'

She touched his arm; her hand was cold as stone. 'Eochaidh King of Tara, see how the moonlight lies broken around you, like a pitcher of milk spilled on the ground, useless. Be merciful, let Étaín go. Your people follow you gladly now to war, but they'll curse you when they bury their dead.'

'They're glad to go to war for a just cause.'

'It's not for Midhir's gold, then, you brought your warriors?'

'They are to punish Midhir for his crime.'

'And these thousand that you send to war to die for you, will you be glad when their blood soaks the fields below Brí Léith? When the ravens swarm?'

'I have never sent a man into battle without need.'

'Eochaidh King of Tara, you are a young man to seek death. Let the white ravens take you. The king of the sidhe is the man who came to you. He is in his royal fort with the woman. Go there and leave us in peace.'

Eochaidh swung his sword, but it fell on stone, ringing loud. The woman was gone.

Eochaidh said, 'He made a road for me to travel to Brí Léith, and so with these thousand and more I will travel and destroy him.' At his instruction Fedach cut three wands of yew from the forest and carved notches on them. By the use of bodhran and yew wands he confirmed that Étaín was with Midhir in Brí Léith. Then Eochaidh said to his captain, 'Tomorrow we'll go north, to Tara and Dun Fremain, and get men, horses, chariots and weapons, and then west to Brí Léith.' And the word went up in the camp, 'Brí Léith' and it spread like a mountain fire in summer, 'Gold in Brí Léith!'

CHAPTER 5

The Razing of the Sidhe

EOCHAIDH AND HIS ARMY filled the road that Midhir had made, and when they reached Dun Fremain, the sky was black in the northwest. Brí Léith was preparing for war. That day a storm came out of the north. Cattle lay down in the fields and huddled against the banks of furze, and the wind blew, breaking trees, and destroying the wattled huts around the fort. Rain came down hard, swelling the creeks to muddy, fast moving lakes, running thigh-deep across the fields. But the storm passed quickly over Dun Fremain, and stars came out while the torrents still ran over the fields.

The next morning not a leaf remained on the trees, and Eochaidh sent his army along the wooded road to Brí Léith with no fear of ambush. Chariots, horses, men and carts with battering rams and slings moved over the planked road, wide enough for two chariots to pass, and dark flood water rushed below on both sides of the road. When the army reached the track that wound up Brí Léith the bare-limbed woods were quiet. There were no cattle in the pastures or byres. The huts were empty.

They camped below the first rampart, out of range of spears and stones. Their horses neighed and were answered within the fort. That night the smoke from the campfires mingled with smoke from the fort; the cloud passed above Brí Léith and dissolved over the bog.

Morning came and Ailill made his report to Eochaidh.

'Has Midhir slaughtered his own cattle? Before it was light I walked close to the wall and heard nothing. It's a poor man we go against.'

'The wealth of Midhir is in gold, not in men or cattle,' said Eochaidh.

'If there's no gold in Brí Léith the army will be gone at the first snow,' said Ailill.

'There will be nothing left of Brí Léith by the first snow.'

That day Eochaidh burned all the houses and the byres, and his army began to dig out the rath wall. Stones, spears and boiling water rained down on them. Eight men were killed and five so badly burned that all wished they would die quickly. But Ailill made a roofed cart to protect the excavation, and by nightfall they had dug a cave under the wall wide enough for a brush fire.

The next morning Eochaidh dressed for battle in his purple tunic, and his barbed iron spears, and he gave orders that the fire be set. The pitch and pine boughs caught quickly. Soon the alder beams that supported the stone wall began to crack and sag, and the wall gave way. Trumpets rang out.

Just inside the fort Eochaidh saw a flash of yellow hair behind a long leather shield bound with bronze. The warrior met him with a barbed bronze spear. Eochaidh hurled his iron spear at the shield; it split the leather and wood beneath but his opponent only shuddered, and stood his ground. The curled iron barbs were hooked fast into the shield. Eochaidh ran forward and stepped hard on the end of his spear that trailed the ground, and his weight pulled down the shield. He struck the man with his long axe on the top of his head and split his head down to the shoulder. Blood rained on Eochaidh; and a cry of triumph started from him, but then he saw that it was not Midhir.

He turned, wiping blood from his eyes, and swung his axe wide, cutting the sword arm straight off a young boy who was locked bronze to iron with a guard. He turned from one weapon to another, cutting and smashing leather, wood, bronze, muscle and bone, keeping his balance as he would on a green horse, in a curragh on rough water, feeling the fallen bodies under him without looking, but avoiding them still, and keeping his distance from the ditch and the wall.

Suddenly it was quiet, and he stopped, breathing hard, his hands and arms numb. There were no more of Midhir's warriors to fight. It was getting dark. He signalled to his guards to pull the bodies of his own men back through the opening of the wall to their camp. There were no women to keen the dead, but a single bodhran took up a slow rhythm, and kept it going all night.

The next morning Eochaidh rose stiffly from his bed. Before it was light he ordered his men to cut boughs and fill in the ditch before the inner rath, so they could bring ladders to the wall, and enter Midhir's fortress. When his men went through the hole in the first wall, a flock of crows rose screaming from the bodies of Midhir's warriors. Eochaidh's men threw most of the bodies into the ditch, then piled boughs and branches and stones on top. But the youngest fallen they hurled with their machines over the walls into the fort.

For one week they cut down the woods on the sides of Brí Léith. Eochaidh and his army sent spears with shafts of ash and birch into the fort, and arrows tipped with deadly yew. At dusk each night when the fighting ended he cried aloud that he would never stop until Étaín was returned to him, and Brí Léith would be destroyed so that no one would ever again think that they could steal without punishment.

One evening there was a singer on the other side of the wall, and the song went on all night, over and over.

'Étaín and Midhir sleep within.
Eochaidh and his men
Will rot on the mountainside.
To the King of Tara and his men,
Death comes soon
On the sides of Brí Léith.
The raven tells it,
Who eats the dead
Knows the truth of my song.'

But the next day Eochaidh's men broke the inner rath and gained the fort. They took Midhir's horses that were hobbled beside the mound, their ribs sharp under their winter coats. They found oats, and open pits with the bones of cattle and pigs in the bottom, but little food. The house was empty.

The entrance to the great mound under the house was closed. The men began to pull the stones away, looking for gold under each rock. The mound was surrounded with deeply buried, slanted rocks, so sharp and close together that a horse or ox couldn't approach it, and the men had to work alone. At the end of the day little progress had been made.

At nightfall a guard was set around the mound, and the army camped in the shelter of the two raths, for winter had come, and the wind froze the men's hands and feet. The next morning the guards were dead, every one of them with a barbed bronze spear in him, and the stones that had been pulled from the entrance were restored.

The clouds were the colour of iron and the wind fierce that day while Eochaidh's men worked moving stones. But the next morning again Eochaidh found his guards dead, and the barricade repaired. He set all that remained of his army to remove the stones, but when night came he could get no one to watch. Toward morning snow began to fall. Eochaidh went to the mound, his guards with him. As he approached the entrance, he was struck in the shoulder by two white ravens; they perched on the wall behind him. Then two white wolves came out of the passage, and sat in the snow, watching him. He left the mound and went to the camp, and told his plan.

'I will grant to any man who has fought before the fort of Brí Léith the right to dig a mound for its gold and to kill the people of Midhir wherever he finds them. But when spring comes I'll summon you, and we'll fight the enemy until Brí Léith falls and Étaín and Midhir's gold belong again to our people.' And his army was satisfied, saying they had a strong king.

Each spring and summer Eochaidh led them to war against the people of the sidhe, and many cairns were destroyed. After two winters there were no swans nesting in Ireland, but the fortress of Midhir stood; Brí Léith could not be taken or destroyed.

When all the cairns in the north had been ransacked and broken, Eochaidh went south again to Slievenamon. It was winter, and there was thick furred frost on the thorn trees when Eochaidh climbed the path to the top, where the cairn faced the low winter sun. It was more than fifteen years since he had last climbed the mountain. He ordered his men to pull away the threshold stones of the cairn. That night the woman came to their hearth fire.

'If you wake the ten times ten thousand bats on Slievenamon, they will starve and die, and plague will come on you and your people. Why have you come here again?' she asked. 'What is our crime against you? Thousands have died and more have suffered for you.'

'Tell me how to get inside Brí Léith.'

'If I tell you, will you leave this mountain?'

'I will.'

'You swear it; it is your word?'

'I swear.'

'Put blind dogs and blind cats before the mound at Brí Léith, and they'll warn you when Midhir and his people come and go from the mound.' Then she disappeared.

Before they left the mountain the next morning Eochaidh told his men to pull apart the cairn, and look for gold. But when they stepped into the passage, there was a stirring and fluttering deep inside, and bats poured from the cairn.

There was no gold on Slievenamon. There was nothing in the mound but dead bats who some sound of wind or passing animal had waked, and waking, couldn't sleep again for hunger. Perhaps they had gone out to search for gnats or flowers but finding nothing but bare branches, had come back inside to starve and slowly die, falling at last from the roof of the cairn.

Spring came and Eochaidh paid gold to raise an army for Brí Léith; it was fifty thousand strong when they covered the road from Tara to Midhir's fort. But this year they were met in battle on the plain before Brí Léith, and Midhir's own son, a boy with gold helmet and chariot drawn by two white stallions, led his army against Eochaidh. At the end of the first day the boy was carried back to the mountain in a cart; one of Eochaidh's chariots had been driven up against him, and over him, and his body was dragged for a long time by frightened horses over the bog. On the third day of battle chariots could no longer cross the fields for the number of dead left there.

After that no army came out of Brí Léith to Eochaidh, and he sent his men up the mountain, and they pulled the stones away from the mound. Just before dusk Eochaidh left a cat and dog whose eyes he had blinded before the mound, and he set a watch. Night came and soon the dog growled. Eochaidh saw Midhir come out of the mound, carrying the body of his son. He showed himself, and Midhir stopped.

'What have you lost these years, Eochaidh, that your own hair has turned white?'

'You know better than anyone, Midhir. I have no children to mourn; my wife was stolen from me.'

'Go home, Eochaidh. Let me bury my son.'

'You won't keep her,' said Eochaidh.

'Go home. The woman you desire will meet you at Tara tomorrow. Will that satisfy you?'

'It will,' said Eochaidh.

'Swear before these men, and my dead child, you won't make war against me.'

Eochaidh cut his arm with the blade of his spear and let the blood drip on the grass. 'I swear.'

Midhir sighed, brushing the hair back from the boy's face. 'Tomorrow there will be more guests satisfied on my fields than ever came to Uisnech, in the days when the Daghdha served from his cauldron that was never empty. Tomorrow there will be crows on the fields feasting, and the wolves won't cry at night for hunger.' Then two white ravens came out of the mound, and the two white wolves after, and settled beside Midhir, sniffing the boy he carried. 'They are called Sorrow and Spirit, and their mother is the Hag of the Sidhe. She'll greet you tomorrow, but you have nothing to fear from her. When you've taken the woman, she will let me know.'

At dawn Eochaidh and his men rode to Tara. From a distance they saw a crowd gathered on the Mound of the Hostages. The day was bright and the yellow hair of fifty young women caught the sun like a field of primroses. As Eochaidh climbed the hill, an old woman met him halfway. Her back was bent and she walked slowly, but with vigour. Grey hair clung to her head like leaves on an oak in winter; her blue eyes were mottled with amber cloud. There were gold armlets on her soft wrinkled arms, and a large gold pin holding a purple cloak on her shoulders. She looked straight at Eochaidh, with no fear of him. Her voice was rough. 'Welcome, Eochaidh, High King of Tara. You of all men are known to me.

'Now you must choose your bride. Choose carefully but quickly. We must set out soon for home. They're not for your slaves or your bravest warrior.'

He walked among them, looking at each woman's face with the wind blowing their capes and hair, but to Eochaidh no woman looked more like Étaín than another. He was ashamed and afraid to face his men.

'But I am the true King of Tara,' he said, 'and I will know Étaín by her serving. Bring tables and pitchers of drink to the Mound of the Hostages. Bring them quickly, and I'll show you Étaín, rescued by my hand, and yours, from the sidhe.'

Then Eochaidh led the women to the tables, and he stood beside each one as she poured him out of a cup of ale. And as each poured he looked at her face, and her body, and touched her thigh or back, whatever part pleased him, and finally he came to the last two women. He gave one the pitcher and when she looked up at him, taking it, he saw that her eyes were blue, and her skin white as bleached bone, and her lips red as hawthorn berries. He put his hands on her hips as she tilted the pitcher toward the cup, and she stopped. She turned to the woman beside her, saying, 'His hunger is like a beast, so he must be served like a beast,' and she let the ale spill into her hand above the cup. She turned to him, the ale dripping from her cupped hands, and he drank from her hands.

'What is your name?' he asked.

'Étaín Esa,' she answered him.

'This is Étaín,' Eochaidh cried out, 'although she's not herself.' Ailill agreed, 'It is surely Étaín, though she has lived captive in the sidhe, and her ways are strange.' The rest of the women went down the hill, and Eochaidh's guards conducted them to the western road.

That night and for one week after there was celebration in Tara. The poets sang of Eochaidh's wisdom, and his martial skills, and the way he taught men how to harness an ox at the shoulder to pull four times the weight of one bound at the neck; for only Eochaidh and Ailill knew that it was Midhir who had invented that way of working.

Eochaidh lived in peace at Tara for several years, and one spring day he was sitting in the courtyard before the hall with his wife, who was heavy with child, and they were talking. Without warning Midhir stood before them, and the girl rose smiling, giving her hand to him.

'Are you well, Eochaidh?' asked Midhir, taking her hand in his own.

'I am.'

'You didn't play the game fairly,' he said. 'You put great hardship on me. I did nothing to harm you.'

'I didn't give you my wife,' said Eochaidh. 'She was stolen from me.'

'But now you're satisfied.'

'I am,' he said, rising, putting his arm around the girl's shoulders.

'You want nothing from me?'

'Nothing.'

'Then answer me; is your mind at ease?'

'It is,' he answered, walking with Étaín back to the bench.

'So is mine,' said Midhir. 'Your wife was pregnant when she was taken from you, and she bore a daughter, and it is she who sits beside you. Your wife is with me, and you yourself have let her go a second time.'

Eochaidh didn't move from the bench. He watched Midhir walk down the steps until he was out of sight, and then he left the girl and went to his tent.

When the woman who was called Étaín bore him a child, it was a girl. Eochaidh said, 'I swear by the gods my people swear by, I and my daughter's daughter shall never look on one another,' and he ordered two men of his court to take the baby out of Tara and destroy it. When the baby was taken, Étaín disappeared from the court. Eochaidh did not look for her.

He went then to Dun Fremain. He would not return to Tara; but lived in Dun Fremain and made war on the hostages who had escaped from Tara, and people said that his mind was troubled. Then a grandson of Midhir, a man named Sigmall Cael, allied himself with one of the hostages of Meath, and together they burned Dun Fremain, and brought Eochaidh's head to Brí Léith, for the honour of Midhir.

But Midhir sent it back to Tara, and the druids made a ceremony of burial for him, putting the burned bones in the Brugh. And the people said it was hard to find a man without some madness in him, and maybe it wouldn't be a bad thing to live without a high king.

EPILOGUE

IT WAS WINTER when Midhir and Étaín Echraide sat on a curbstone at the Brugh. They played the funeral game with chalk marbles on the carved stone, capturing them from one another as they moved into one spiral and out again into another. They had searched all morning among the piles of white quartz which Eochaidh's men had pulled down from the entrance of the Brugh, but had finally found enough marbles for the game. The pasture grass flowed under the wind like a green river winding alongside the blue Boyne, and Étaín's yellow hair rose and fell with the gusts. When a heron swept the top of the long grass with his slow, great wings, they both stopped and watched him fly along the river.

They played without talking, thinking of Eochaidh. The ash of his bones lay neatly in the cupped basin within the farthest chamber of the Brugh, that which they call the Lake of Two Stones. It was for his sake they played, easing him from one world to the next with their game. When the game ended they sat awhile looking at the river, at the white clouds changing their shapes in the wind. Then Étaín touched Midhir's sleeve and they took the marbles inside and made a pile of them under the bowl, so that Eochaidh's spirit might use them to pass the time.

Then they lay down in the chamber, and they loved each other, their breath loud in the cave where the wind's roar never comes. They slept then, and when they woke Étaín touched his hair, and kissed his mouth and his eyes, and then she lay beside him with her hand in his and she sang in the dark,

'Let him rest.
Let his death-anger leave the stones.
Let him leave the minds of people who loved him.
Let him go in peace where the wind takes him.
Let his seed be planted and thrive.'

After a silence Midhir said, 'He destroyed himself and the land about him. It's a hard thing to wish.'

'His daughter Esa brought you a hundred cattle from Tara when she left him.'

'It was little compensation for the theft of her child.'

'The child lives; still I could have kept Esa from Eochaidh,' said Étaín.

'To have slept with her father was no shame to her, not knowing him. She went willingly to the bed of the High King of Tara. I saw the love between them, before I destroyed it. It's I who have the weight of shame in this, knowing what would come, letting my own death be a spur to get you to my side.'

'And I, not making a choice, letting winter and summer pass knowing I loved you.'

'I've closed the door to Dowth. I was watched, walking there.'

'What is it like there?' she whispered.

'Like a grave half made. Like a badger's lair that a bear has plundered, and finding nothing, destroyed in his rage. Some of the carved stones broken.'

'And Knowth?'

'That is safely hidden below their own fort. And their ashes lie here; this mound they won't destroy. But we are scattered like the white stones of the Brugh, our people lost. We can't search openly, as a man might look for a calf on his horse. We come to the cave in secret, and hide in the dark.'

'Midhir, it is not so dark now. Look at the stones, at the floor of the passageway. The sun is coming in, Midhir. The stones burn with its fire. I know this place.'

They stood in the chamber and watched the light. When it began to dim again, Midhir put his arms around Étaín, and held her close, then he took her hand and she followed him down the narrow passage, past the stones with their waves and wings and spinning clouds. They went out of the mound; the sun was clear of the hills before them. They crossed the field, and went down to the river Boyne.

Midhir and Étaín walked into the river, past an otter lacing the reeds with his sleek stroke, and they stood where the water was thigh-deep, braced against the pull of the current that moved to the sea. And all around them the river moved in fine waves, wind and stones and reeds making lines that broke and joined in feathers, arrows, coils, silver and gold where the sun touched it. Étaín dipped back into the river, letting her hair flow back over the surface. Underwater the long grass tangled around her thighs and lower legs, around her ankles, and she shook free, gliding out over the broken surface of the river, and turned to Midhir, his head bowed, his white wings curved and they drifted together along the shore below the Brugh.

Historical Note

Daughter of the Boyne is based on the Old Irish epic, The Wooing of Etain, one of the chief mythological cycles of early Irish literature. Portions of the epic are preserved in the manuscript Lebor na Huidre, but for years scholars debated the goddess Étaín's fate in the first and final parts of the story for only the middle section was complete. Examining medieval Irish manuscripts in the Phillipps Collection at Cheltenham, Dr. R.I. Best recognized some parchment as part of the Yellow Book of Lecan. Apparently the folio numbers had been erased in order to hide the fact that the manuscript was a fragment. These lost leaves contained the complete text of Tochmarc Étaíne or The Wooing of Etain. The whole text was published in *Eriu xii*, with translation, by Dr. Best and Dr. Osborn Bergin in 1937.

The Game

The game described in this novel is inspired by a definition in The Dictionary of the Irish Language, Royal Irish Academy; 'fid-ciall' as 'wood-intelligence', the ogham alphabet and the 'Cad Goddeu', trans. Patrick Ford, 1977, as well as from early known uses of trees.

Eoin MacWhite, *'Early Irish Board Games'* and H.J.R. Murray, *A History of Board Games*, Hacker: New York, 1978, suggest that fidchell may have resembled a simple Roman board game, ludus latrunculorum; however, there is insufficient evidence in the manuscripts to make an indisputable case. At present, fidchell remains a mystery.

My Time in the War
Romie Lambkin
A captivating diary of an Irish woman in World War II. Adventure and excitement among the young soldiers in battle-scarred Europe.
paperback £7.99

On Borrowed Ground
Hugh Fitzgerald Ryan
'Beautifully written, subtle, uplifting, a novel of an Irish writer come of age.' Benedict Kiely
paperback £4.99

The Kybe
Hugh Fitzgerald Ryan
'The first thing that strikes the reader about this remarkable first novel, is the agreeable clarity with which it is written.'
Irish Independent
paperback £3.50

The Café Cong
Niall Quinn
'There are few writers who have captured so well the disintegration of Irishness in the birth of a new international underclass.' Fintan O'Toole, *Sunday Tribune*
paperback £7.95

Stolen Air
Niall Quinn
'One of the most interesting and provocative Irish novels I've read in a long time.' *Books Ireland*
paperback £3.95 / hardback £9.95

Dark Paradise
Catherine Brophy
'Brophy's fiction explores the perennial theme of civilisation versus nature with intelligence, passion and grace.'
Irish Press
paperback £4.99

Thy Neighbour's Wife
Liam O'Flaherty
O'Flaherty's famous first novel. A powerful and passionate story of an island priest's conflict between religion and love.
paperback £5.99

Mr. Gilhooley
Liam O'Flaherty
'A great writer unique in any language, any culture.... He has all the potential for becoming a matrix for the yearnings of another generation.' Neil Jordan, *Hot Press*
paperback £4.99

Famine
Liam O'Flaherty
'Famine is worthy of its author and of the whole corpus of contemporary Irish fiction ... it is the kind of truth that only a major writer of fiction is capable of portraying.' Anthony Burgess, *Irish Press*
paperback £5.99

Short Stories
Liam O'Flaherty
'A satisfying choice ... compels belief ... never wavers for a single phrase.' *Times Literary Supplement*
paperback £4.99